D0383803

Dear Mystery Reader:

Are you ready for food, fun, and a little bit of murder? Then settle in for a mystery served up Heaven Lee-style.

This time Lou Jane Temple takes her delightful Kansas City crew on the road for a romp through the celebrity ski world of Aspen, Colorado. From across the globe, the cream of the culinary crop have come for the annual Best Chef contest. And while the food is truly delicious, the competition gets a bit vicious when contestants find themselves knee-deep in murder.

You'll find Lou Jane's recipes just as delicious as her mysteries. The book in your hands is full of tasty fare. And once you've steered through its scrumptious dishes, you'll have to check out *Death by Rhubarb* and *Revenge of the Barbeque Queens* for more, including two of my personal favorites: Gingerbread Upside-Down Cake and Viet Summer Rolls. Yum!

Heaven Lee mysteries are selling like hotcakes. Lou Jane's clearly building a legion of loyal fans, all hungry for more from their favorite culinary sleuth. *A Stiff Risotto* won't let them down. And keep your eye out for the next Heaven Lee mystery. Lou Jane's already cooking up another delectable page-turner.

Yours in crime,

Joe Veltre
St. Martin's Dead Letter Paperback Mysteries

Heaven slipped away. She remembered seeing trucks backed up to an opening on the south side. When Heaven got there, she ducked down and slipped under the canvas. Even though the sun was bright outside, the interior of the tent was dim. But still Heaven could tell something was terribly wrong.

The chairs, normally in tidy, neat rows were thrown helter skelter. The walls of the tent were scrawled with graffiti and epithets in English, Italian, and Spanish. The letters were written in something red. The demonstration area was demolished. A mirror, normally placed over the work table so the participants could see the hands of the chef, was smashed and jagged pieces of glass were scattered about. The food processor looked as if someone had taken a sledgehammer to it. A refrigerator had been pushed off the stage and the contents thrown all over. The sheet pans with the chilled risotto were scattered everywhere. On one of the pans the shape of a body had been carved out of rice. A long French kitchen knife was sticking out of a sign advertising Sergio's appearance. The word "die" had been scrawled across Sergio's picture.

A STIFF RISOTTO

Lou Jane Temple

St. Martin's Paperbacks

A STIFF RISOTTO

Copyright © 1997 by Lou Jane Temple.

ISBN: 0-312-96321-1

Printed in the United States of America

St. Martin's Paperbacks edition/October 1997

10 9 8 7 6 5 4 3 2 1

To my dear friend Greg Smith, who
sat me down and turned on the computer.

In real life, there is a great event in Aspen, Colorado every June. It is the *Food and Wine* Magazine Classic and it gave me the inspiration for my spoof. If you love food and/or wine, there is no better event anywhere. I thank the magazine staff for their help.

Special thanks to Tim Handley and his Aspen posse who extended their friendship to me. Thanks also to Mary Eshbaugh Hayes, the Jerome Hotel, the Aspen Ski Co., and the Caribou Club.

My Kansas City friends Fred and Lillis Beihl lent me their home in Aspen so I could do research, and for that I am grateful.

I also want to thank newspaper columnist Charles Ferruza, who retired the name of his column, "The Real Dish," so I could use it.

A STIFF
RISOTTO

ONE

LINDA Lunch had heartburn. It was that new little twerp in the test kitchen. The girl didn't know a jalapeño from a habañero. Linda suspected the new test cook might even have slipped hot chilies in the mango salsa on purpose. Just because Linda had commented in a negative vein about the lemon tart the so-called chef had served last Friday. Linda recalled she had said something about it being the most vile thing she had ever put in her mouth.

"She's obviously passive aggressive," Linda muttered as she popped another Tums. She just wouldn't go to the daily noon tasting anymore. She couldn't afford to get sick. She had too much to do before she left for Aspen.

The Real Dish Aspen Festival was her chance to shine each year. As editor of *The Real Dish* magazine, she was in charge of one of the most prestigious events in the world of food. Famous chefs rearranged their schedules when Linda asked them to do a cooking demonstration in Aspen. Winemakers from around the world flocked to the tiny town with cases of their best wines, actually eager to give out samples. High-income foodies swept in from all over the country and from abroad to rub elbows with Marcella Hazan, Julia Child, Jacques Pepin, and the like. If things didn't go right, it would reflect on her. So Linda Lunch would just have to make sure things went perfectly. She picked up the phone and dialed an internal number.

"Tab, get in here," she snapped. "I want to go over the whole event again, top to bottom. Yes, darling. I know we just did that this morning, but I'm concerned about the wine seminars. I don't think we have showcased the guy from Italy enough, yeah, Antonori, or whatever his name is. I think we need to give him a little luncheon, maybe on Sunday, after the awards ceremony. We'll need to make reservations at the Ritz, or maybe at Taka-Sushi. What do you mean you're busy with the copy editors? Get in here before I send you back to *Better Homes and Gardens* or better yet, get in here before I tell everyone your real name." Linda slammed the phone down with satisfaction. That got him every time.

In ten seconds flat, Harlin Garner, aka Tab, was standing at her door. "You've got a lot of nerve talking about changing names, Ms. Lunch," he parried valiantly. "I happen to know your paychecks are made out to Linda Lubavich."

Tab had held his own as Linda's personal assistant longer than anyone in *Real Dish* history: two years, four months, and twenty-two days. Just hold on a few more days, he told himself. He sat down and pulled the computer printout of the festival activities out of his tote.

Linda snatched the calendar from Tab's hands and slinked back into her oversized gray leather chair. "Yes, and those paychecks are absolutely enormous, as you also know. Speaking of money, who are you betting on for Best Chef of the Year?" Linda asked absently as she started to read the schedule for the hundredth time, red pencil poised.

The staff of the magazine always had a betting pool on who would win the title. It was the New York food-publishing world version of a football pool.

Tab was working on copy for the July issue, and he had brought it along to Linda's office, knowing there would be time to do some editing while Linda went over every comma of the festival schedule again. He looked up from his work. "Well, the way I see it, the old Italian and his son cancel each other out. Number three, the guy from Texas, is a long-shot. We've never had a barbecue cooker in the competition before, and I'm afraid everyone thinks of barbecue as just putting some hotdogs on the grill. I don't think they'll take him seriously. Candidate number four is the Louisiana chef, Ernest Laveau. Susan Spicer from New Orleans won last year, so I don't think the Cajun guy has a chance this year. The voters like something new, like the new Floribbean cuisine. I put my ten spot on the Latin woman from Miami, Lola what's her name,'' Tab drawled in his Mississippi twang.

He had lived in New York five years now, but he wouldn't dream of losing his Southern accent. The boys loved it.

"Castro, darling, her last name is Castro, just like the dictator. I'll have to ask her if she's related.'' Linda put down the papers and smiled. "Don't rule Sergio out, honey. He's a crowd favorite. He wrote the first Italian cookbook every gourmet in America bought. And those gourmets are our people. Half of the festival voters learned to make pasta from that damn cookbook, back when pasta was an exotic item. We can't deny the power of loyalty. Sergio has become an icon. He's like an Italian James Beard.''

Tab threw a wad of paper across the desk at Linda. "I know it just kills you, you can't just name a winner yourself, that you have to let the unwashed masses vote for Best Chef.''

"You know me too well, you bitch,'' Linda laughed as she threw the paper wad back at Tab. "This Best Chef of the Year voting dinner was set up before my reign or you can bet a panel of experts would be the only election committee. Experts who would do what I told them. But I'm stuck with allowing the public to vote. And I have to admit the dinner with the nominated chefs each cooking a course is one of the reasons the festival is so popular. Every Tom, Dick, and Harry wants to be in the first five hundred to pay their festival entry so they can go to the dinner and vote for Best Chef.''

Tab wasn't entirely convinced. Linda was too much of a power freak to relinquish control without a fight. "Don't tell me you don't sometimes go down in the mailroom and check out the return addresses. You know, Boston return addresses for a Boston chef? Then, when you get to Aspen, you know the dining room will be packed with hometown fans voting for their hometown chef who also happens to be the one you want to win. I bet you can stack a dining room when you have to."

Linda cackled with delight but there was an edge of malice in her laugh and Tab saw once more why she was feared in the food world. "You better believe it, Tab honey. I always get the results I want, and don't you forget it."

Tab Garner smiled his most dazzling orthodontist-created smile. "How could I? Now who from the press do you want to invite to the breakfast with Julia?"

TWO

HEAVEN Lee had a glazed look in her eyes. She shook her fingers out on both hands, like a secretary at the end of a hard day at the computer. Then she rolled her neck like an athlete working out a muscle spasm. Her bright red hair was pulled back in a ponytail that rotated like a soft propeller on the back of her head. After all the machinations, she looked over their lunch with renewed interest. "Okay, maybe one more piece." Heaven grabbed the platter of fried chicken and fished around for a wishbone. "One of the things I love about this place is the way they cut up their chicken."

Chris Snyder nodded in approval. "They cut it so there's a wishbone, just like my grandmother used to."

"And they have backs. Most restaurants don't fry the bony pieces," Joe Long muttered from the other side of the table, his mouth full. "I must admit I was a little miffed when we had to plan our trip to Colorado around eating at a fried chicken place in the middle of Kansas."

Heaven gave Joe an I-told-you-so look and smugly spooned a big helping of mashed potatoes on her plate, followed by gravy and coleslaw and lots of watermelon pickles. "Oh, ye of little faith. I know that if an uninformed person were so inclined, one could leave their home in Kansas City before dawn and make it to Aspen in one day. But then that poor ignorant soul would be passing through the Salina area at nine or ten in the morning. The Brookville Hotel doesn't have a fried chicken breakfast, although it's not a bad idea. You guys are just lucky you're not traveling with someone like that, ignorant about the good things in life. Pass the cream corn, please.''

Kansas Cream Corn

3 T. butter
1 onion, diced (sweet, if possible)
6 ears of corn, the corn cut off the cob
1 cup heavy cream
1 T. sugar
kosher salt and coarse ground pepper
Options: 2 jalapeños, sliced. A red or green pepper, diced. A homegrown tomato, diced

In a heavy sauté pan, melt the butter and sauté the onion over low heat until it is translucent. Add corn, sugar, and a dash of salt and pepper. Cook ten minutes and add cream, then continue cooking another ten minutes. When the cream has reduced and thickened slightly, add any options. Adjust salt and pepper to taste.

Kansas Coleslaw

2–2½ lb. head of green cabbage
1 cup white vinegar
1 cup heavy cream
⅔ cup sugar
1 tsp. kosher salt

Grate, thinly slice, or shred the cabbage. I personally like this recipe with the cabbage grated but it works all ways. Pour over the cabbage first the vinegar, then the sugar and salt, then the cream. The order is important because if you pour the cream on and then the vinegar, curdling can occur. Let the cabbage sit without stirring for twenty minutes or so before you mix it up. Mix and chill for at least an hour before serving. Two or three hours is better. You can get wild and creative with this recipe by changing the style of vinegar used (rice wine, raspberry, balsamic). But of course, the Kansas way is with white vinegar.

Chris pushed the bowl of corn in Heaven's direction and grabbed more chicken for himself. "I love the generous use of various fats."

"Isn't it great? Don't tell these folks butter and cream are bad for you. When I was a kid growing up on the farm near Council Grove, we drove over here two or three times a year with aunts and uncles and cousins. They've always had the same menu and the same Blue Willow dishes. Of course, we didn't have to come over here to get good food. My mom made fried chicken just as good as this."

"Of course she did," Joe said with a laugh. "We don't think you're a bad daughter if you admit to liking someone else's chicken. After all, your mom's been dead a long time. She wouldn't begrudge you a couple of good crispy wings now and then. She's probably smiling down on our greasy fingers right now."

Heaven looked over the heads of the diners, out the window of the gussied-up old dining room. She could see a row of cottonwood trees, their leaves shining silver in the sun. She pointed outside. "When I was a little girl I could sit outside and just listen to the wind in the cottonwoods. I loved that sound. My mom always hated it. She said if they weren't so tall and didn't block the wind in the winter, she'd have Daddy cut the cottonwoods down. She called the tree music 'that dad-blame racket.' "

Joe threw a huge wad of one-dollar bills on the table. "Don't even think about crying," he said as he grabbed one last chicken leg. He got up, threw his napkin on the table, rolled his eyes at Heaven, and took a big munch on the leg, all at the same time. "We'd better get out of here before we all fall asleep from overeating, and you become too maudlin to travel with. That's about thirty-five dollars, which more than covers the chicken. Leave a tip." Joe was tall and lanky, with dark curly hair and flashing eyes. His body was one of his most useful tools as an actor, and now he turned and walked away from their table with a perfect Charlie Chaplin duck walk. Heaven and Chris threw another fifteen dollars on the table and followed Joe to the car.

Heaven had put the second seat in her van that served as a catering vehicle for Cafe Heaven most of the time. The roomy interior was packed full. There was a cooler of soft drinks and bottled water and another cooler of fruit and candy bars and some brownies that Pauline, the baker at the restaurant, had made for their journey. There were suitcases and a cardboard box with wigs sticking out of it. The two hooks in the back of the van were loaded with garment bags. Not one of the three travelers knew the meaning of packing lightly.

"That place is so great. I'm inspired," Heaven said with a laugh as she jumped up behind the driver's seat. "Those people don't know nothing 'bout no Best Chef contest or Zagat ratings or low-fat cooking. And there's something so right about the experience 'cause they do what they do so well."

"Without any apology, I might add," Chris chimed in. "I wonder what the Brookville Hotel folks would say if they knew where we were headed: to a food and wine festival in a movie star vacation town, where the affluent pay to eat the finest food and drink the finest wine for three days."

Joe snorted. "Yes, this little event is really going to add to the betterment of humankind, isn't it?"

Heaven laughed. "I didn't see either of you having a moral dilemma when the words expense-paid trip to Aspen were mentioned back in Kansas City. Besides, this is a cool event even if the town is a celeb suburb. At least we're going in the summer. It's the off season.''

"Who are you trying to fool?'' Chris asked. "There isn't an off season in Aspen. They have music festivals and think tanks and design conferences and all kinds of shit in the summer. I went two years ago for a playwrights' powwow. David Mamet was there and he never goes anywhere.''

"Well, la-de-David Mamet-da,'' Joe snipped.

Joe and Chris were both performance artists and did traditional theater stuff to boot. Together they produced an open mike night at Cafe Heaven, and this had gotten them and the cafe lots of publicity, sometimes more than they wanted.

Chris did a lot of work with social issues and gay social issues in particular. He had received several grants and writing awards in the last couple of years.

Joe concentrated more on acting and set design. He had worked on three or four films and made-for-TV movies that had been shot in Kansas City.

"Now, kids, don't fight. You'll give Mom a headache and then she'll be cross,'' Heaven said in the voice of Beaver Cleaver's mother. She turned the van back on the interstate heading west. "Maybe we should talk about what we're going to do when it's our turn in Aspen.''

Joe smiled maliciously. "I'd rather talk about Rowland Alexander. Why do you think he asked us to come do this little role-playing session? I'm sure they could have hired local Aspen actors. I think he wants to see you, that's what I think.''

Heaven blushed and glared at Joe. "Nonsense. Rowland has a wife back at the winery in Australia.''

Joe was not easily deterred from his pet theory. "And you have a boyfriend back in Kansas City. So? You know how much Rowland likes to come to Kansas City and give those wine dinners. I bet—''

"Well, don't,'' Heaven interrupted. "You'd lose. Rowland has been in Kansas City on Monday nights at the open mike so he knows you guys are hams. He also knows we can sell wine. If he'd hired actors in Aspen he'd have to write the script and if the actors only knew about jug wine, he'd also have to teach them about wine. With us he gets two for one.''

"A little defensive, are we?" Joe said archly. "Really, I know you care for Hank. Who wouldn't?"

Chris agreed. "Yeah, who couldn't fall for a gorgeous Asian doctor without a mean bone in his body?"

"God, you make him sound boring. Hank is nice, but he's also smart and funny and . . .'' Heaven bit her lip.

Joe poked her in the side. "This is where you say, 'I know that when he gets done with his residency, he'll go off and marry someone his own age' blah-blah.''

"Although I've never heard Hank mention this plan of action," Chris pointed out.

"Well, he is only four years older than my daughter. I think it's reasonable to assume he'll want his own family someday.''

"Not everyone wants a family," Joe pointed out. "Look at us.''

"Speak for yourself," Chris interjected. "I'd love to adopt a kid if they'd just let me.''

Heaven smiled. "You'd make a great dad, Chris. I guess that's the point. So would Hank. He's so good.''

"Heaven," Joe said, "just because you and Jason couldn't make it work, I think you're scared.''

Heaven chuckled. "If you recall, I did have four husbands before Jason and only one of them made me a widow. I think that's the kind of record that can make a girl gunshy, doubt her own ability to commit. No doubt about it though, Jason was a tough one to lose. The restaurant just takes so much time and . . .''

"And I haven't heard Hank complaining," Chris said. "I think you found the solution. Just get someone who works more than you, like a resident physician, and they won't even notice you're never at home. Maybe you should just work your way through the med center.''

Heaven tried to look outraged, but she was laughing along in a minute. "Stop it, you guys. Really. Chris, reach back in that big paisley bag of mine, with the newspaper and the hair dryer sticking out of the top. Find the legal pad with 'How to Not Sell Wine' written on it."

"Got it," Chris said as he twisted around and dumped the bag on his lap. "Why the negative instead of the positive?"

Heaven glanced over her shoulder. "I thought that would be the angle. We would show all the mistakes that servers and restaurants make."

Joe chimed in, "Oh boy, fun. Now I see why you told us to bring the wigs and costumes. Can I be the snotty wine steward?"

THREE

HEAVEN pulled the van up to the gate.

"Whoa, you didn't tell us we were staying behind a moat," Chris said with a low whistle. Joe was the navigator, reading from a hand-drawn map. In spite of several wrong turns on mountain terrain, he had managed to get them to the Aspen vacation home of Peter Cooper, the shopping center mogul of Kansas City. Peter was a fan of Heaven's cafe and had offered her his house because no self-respecting mogul would be caught dead in Aspen in June. The unwritten law had it that if you were a regular, it wasn't cool to be seen in Aspen until July 4.

The map had led them to a perch high above the narrow valley the town of Aspen was snuggled in. The view of the little town was spectacular. Heaven put the van in park and opened the door. "He said the key would be at the guard's gate," she said as she hopped out. At that same moment a young man came out of the office. Tan, muscular but slim, sun-bleached long hair. Very cute in a hunky, ski-bum sort of way, Heaven thought.

"Hi there, can I help you?" he asked.

Heaven explained that they were guests of Peter Cooper and the guard ambled over to the van and peeked in at the guys. They smiled like a couple of Cheshire cats. Heaven winked at them to let them know they had been caught.

He went back inside the office and picked up a manila envelope, then came to the doorway and leaned toward Heaven. "Ms. Lee," he said looking down at the name on the envelope, "could I see some identification? It's our policy not to hand over the keys to someone's home without photo ID. You understand, the residents here pay for privacy and security."

Heaven was ready for this. Her name, of course, was really Katherine O'Malley Martin McGuinne Wolff Steinberg Kelley. Heaven Lee was a name she thought up when she became a stripper for a few weeks, a couple of decades ago. "Heaven Lee is my business name. But you can see the photograph is me," Heaven cooed as she handed him her driver's license. She prayed the kid had enough sense not to start laughing when he saw her birth date. Hopefully he couldn't subtract without a calculator.

The kid was a pro. He just smiled. "Thank you, Ms. Lee. Would you and the other guests mind signing in now? Then when you enter the complex each time, we'll ask for your signature. It's kind of like comparing a check signature."

Heaven, Chris, and Joe passed around a clipboard, each put their John Hancocks on a signature card with the words "Peter Cooper Guests" on the top. Then the guard handed Heaven the manila envelope with her name on it. "Here is the key and a note from Mr. Cooper. Allow me to give you my card. Please call the office if you have any problems. Mr. Cooper's house is the second from the top of the mountain."

Joe called playfully from the passenger's side, "Who's on top, Trixie Malone?" Everyone in the country knew the movie star had a home in Aspen.

The guard gave a little smile. "Normally, the names of the residents are not something we discuss, but I guess Mr. Cooper told you about his famous neighbor. Yes, the top house is Miss Malone's. I trust you not to take advantage of that knowledge?"

Joe was practically jumping up and down in his chair. "Of

course not. We already knew.'' Chris kicked the back of his friend's seat.

Heaven took the envelope and handed it to Joe. ''We already knew. Yeah, right. You two are jumping up and down like you just won the lottery. Do not, I repeat, do not bother Trixie Malone this weekend, no matter what clever tack you come up with. It would be so embarrassing to be asked to leave before Monday.''

Chris piped up from the back, ''I won't do anything stupid, I promise. Isn't this exciting, though? You always read about Aspen being home of the stars and here we're going to be neighbors to one of the biggest. Not that she doesn't look good with that extra twenty pounds.''

Heaven laughed. ''You are cruel. That's what happens when you stop doing cocaine. She was too skinny anyway.''

''We're here,'' Joe said as they pulled down a lane marked Cooper. They stopped in front of a huge log cabin, a log cabin the size of a high school.

''At least it's not one of those ugly postmodern things we passed on the way up here,'' Chris sniffed.

''What a snob,'' Heaven said as she got out of the car and stretched her arms. ''I guess you'd high-tail it back home if we had to stay in one of those ugly postmodern jobs, eh?''

Heaven grabbed a couple of suitcases and followed Joe into the house. It had all the usual grand lodge trappings and more: logs instead of sheet rock, an Andy Warhol on one wall, a Jasper Johns on the other, and a stuffed moose head in the middle. There was a huge vaulted ceiling, a Viola Frey sculpture, a long oriental runner—and that was just the entryway. The whole other side of the house seemed to be made of glass.

''Ah, yes,'' Heaven said. ''Home, sweet home.''

Chris and Joe finished bringing the extensive inventory from the car in the house. ''Mr. Cooper suggests in his note we use any of the bedrooms on the upper levels. That's levels in the plural. I think we'll go on a recon mission, as Jumpin'

Jack would say,'' Joe called as he and Chris headed up the winding log stairs.

Jumpin' Jack was a denizen of 39th Street in Kansas City, where Cafe Heaven was located. Jack thought he was a veteran of Vietnam so he dressed and acted accordingly on occasion. The fact that no branch of the armed forces had ever deemed Jack fit for the stresses of combat did not deter him from this mindset. "Mentioning Jack made me miss home for a second,'' Heaven said out loud to no one. "I hope they don't get in too much trouble while we're gone. I'll have to call later.''

Heaven poked around until she found the restaurant-strength kitchen and was busy investigating the top-of-the-line kitchen gadgets when Joe and Chris found her.

"The Robo-Coupe here is a better model than the one at the cafe, and they only live here two months of the year,'' Heaven said indignantly.

"Don't even think of boosting the Robo-Coupe,'' Joe admonished in a severe tone of voice.

"We put you in the burnt sienna room with a collection of Phillip Mayberry and Adrian Saxe ceramics,'' Chris informed Heaven.

"Those artists use all those patterns and colors. Wasn't there anything more restful?'' Heaven whined.

"Would you rather have the room with all the Northwest Coast burial masks?'' Chris asked with menace in his tone. "I took the Plains Indian room and Joe went for the Art Deco posters. I must say they have pretty good taste for rich people.''

"OK, OK. I get the picture,'' Heaven said. "Modern ceramic versus old ju-ju, I guess I'll sleep better with the modernists. Show me the way. I'm giving us fifteen minutes to freshen up, as they say. We'll go down to town and get our registration packs and I'm meeting Rowland for lunch and you can explore if you want.''

"Oh brother, oh brother,'' Joe whooped. "I love the way you stuck lunch with Rowland in there between registration packs and exploring. Tried to slip it in quietly, didn't you?"

"And we're not invited?" Chris asked.

"Get out of here, you two. Be ready to leave in fifteen minutes. Where do I go?" Heaven asked again.

"Follow us," Chris said. "You won't believe the master bedroom. No, don't say it. Of course, we know better than to sleep in Mr. Cooper's room, but there's a lap pool outside the door that looks like it's suspended in mid-air and the room has every gym thing known to man."

"Oh, and in the note, Peter apologizes that the maid and the yard man are just on half days until July. They work from nine to one, Monday through Friday," Joe added, waving their letter from Peter Cooper under Heaven's nose.

Heaven snatched the letter away and threw it over her shoulder grandly as they walked up the wide log staircase. It floated down to the floor like a paper hanky. "I don't think we can survive," Heaven exclaimed sarcastically. "The staff is just on half days? And how will we ever manage by ourselves on the weekend?"

Joe rolled his eyes in Heaven's direction once more. "Come on, Scarlett, here's your room."

FOUR

MURRAY Steinblatz was worried. He was sure nothing would go wrong, but still, being left in charge of Cafe Heaven had given him a sleepless night. When he was nervous, Murray got hungry. At the crack of dawn he had gone to the Corner Restaurant and wolfed down a porker: eggs, potatoes, sausage and cheese, a pair of banana pancakes, a mango yogurt smoothie, pumpernickel toast, and coffee on the side. After all that and speed reading two newspapers, the *Kansas City Star* and *The New York Times*, he headed for Thirty-ninth Street, to make sure the morning shift was all present and accounted for.

Murray slipped in the back door, right into the kitchen. There was a mild morning breeze outside; inside it was already as steamy as noonday. "Pauline, have you been baking bread all night? This place is already an oven."

Pauline Kramer glared at Murray. "Funny, Murray. A little baking humor there? I am not responsible for the temperature of this place. It's only eight-thirty. The bread is still in its second rise and the pie crust is still resting and the brownie batter is in this bowl. It's hot in here because the air conditioner stopped working."

Brian Hoffman, the lunch chef and day-prep man, looked up from skinning salmon. "It's just as hot out in the dining room. You better do something, man. Lunch will be a disaster.''

Just then Robbie Lunstrom came back in the kitchen from the alley. Robbie was the third member of the day team at the cafe, playing clean-up dish man, shrimp peeler, and general fix-it trouble shooter. Robbie had a smudge of grease on his face, along with a worried look. ''I went up on the roof, to see if it was something obvious. I can break down my dishwasher and replace darn near every part of it. But this air conditioner, I'm stumped, Murray. I've got the phone number of the refrigeration company in the office. I'll go call.'' With that he went through the swinging doors that led to the dining room and the office beyond.

''It does this every summer,'' Pauline commented in an accusatory tone.

Brian nodded knowingly. ''Yeah, man, those flat roofs really hold the heat. The unit is up there and meltdown occurs.'' He slammed some garlic with the side of a Chinese cleaver for emphasis.

Murray jumped. ''Why does this have to happen when Heaven leaves town? What if it needs a new motor or something that costs a lot? She'll kill me.''

Pauline stopped being irritated for a minute and tried to smile soothingly at Murray. ''It usually only costs three or four hundred dollars. The accountant can sign a check in a pinch. And Heaven can be unreasonable sometimes, but she certainly won't blame you for the old, ratty air conditioner. Don't panic yet, Murray.''

Murray winced. '' 'Don't panic yet'? That's supposed to make me feel better? I'll feel better if you volunteer to be the one to tell Heaven when she calls. I'm going to talk this over with Sal,'' he said and went out the back door wringing his hands. Murray had never gotten used to all the disasters that could occur in a restaurant in any twenty-four hour period. He wasn't a true food professional. Really, he was a journalist.

Murray had grown up in Kansas City and gone on to the

Big Apple where he had gained a considerable reputation for his crime reporting. Then disaster struck. Murray's own wife was killed in a hit-and-run accident by a car full of juvenile delinquents. Soon after, Murray quit his job at *The New York Times* and moved back to Kansas City. He was sure he'd never be able to write about crime with any objectivity again. Soon he decided he couldn't write about anything. For more than a year he'd done nothing. When Cafe Heaven opened, Murray asked for a job. He didn't know why, but he had, and Heaven saw fit to find one for him. Six years working the door at Cafe Heaven had brought him partially back to life, but he was still fragile and a little jumpy. Right now, he needed Sal to calm him down.

Every major boulevard, in cities big and small, has one business that is the heart of the street. On Thirty-ninth Street in Kansas City, Sal's Barber Shop is it. Sal d'Giovanni had been cutting hair on Thirty-ninth Street longer than even he could remember. If there was even the hint of news in the city, Sal could weasel it out of the next unsuspecting haircutting client, most of whom ran businesses or institutions around town. Bankers, TV newsmen, and bartenders all made their way to Sal's chair. Now Murray crossed the street and opened the door of the barber shop. Sal was giving a priest a military-style buzz cut.

"Morning, Father. Hey, Sal." He went to the coffee pot and poured some of the inky stuff in one of the many mismatched mugs Sal kept around.

Sal kept working and kept his unlit cigar tightly clamped in his mouth. He didn't even seem to be checking Murray out. "So what's the matter with you?"

Murray was relieved that Sal had picked up on his state of mind. He would have had trouble starting from scratch otherwise. "Heaven went out to Colorado to some food and wine wingding. She won't be back till next Tuesday and the air conditioner decides to crap out. It must be eighty-five degrees in there already."

"Wait, wait! What did I miss?" Mona Simpson, proprietor of The City Cat, a cat gift store next to Cafe Heaven, had seen Murray cross the street to Sal's and could tell something was up. As soon as she had been able to get rid of her customer, a woman desperate for a mechanical meowing water dish, she put a "Be Back Soon" sign on the door and headed for Sal's herself.

Murray looked at Mona pitifully. "Heaven's only been gone a day and the air conditioner broke. Robbie called the refrigeration guys."

"Oh," Mona said with disappointment in her voice, "is that all? I thought something really terrible had happened from the look on your face."

Murray was not ready to give up on his crisis quite yet. "Chances are they won't get the air back on by lunch. It will be hot as Hades and no one will stay for lunch, so we'll lose money and what if it costs a fortune to fix?"

Sal piped in. "So make the decision now to close for lunch. Then you won't waste food."

Mona nodded. "Good idea, Sal. That way you cut your losses, Murray. And I guess you didn't know what my father did for a living up in St. Joseph, Missouri, did you now?"

Murray bit. "Air conditioning?"

Mona patted his hand like he was a sick child. "You better believe it. My brother still runs the biggest heating and cooling company in northern Missouri. Heating and cooling is my middle name, Murray. Why, I spent my youth crawling around basements and climbing up on roofs. Dad was real good about that, he didn't make me stay home 'cause I was a girl. In those days fathers and daughters didn't really do much together. Me going to work with Dad on Saturdays was our bonding time, I guess. 'Course, no one knew about bonding in the fifties."

"Thank God," Sal muttered. "My girl did the same thing, Mona. She loved coming down here on Saturdays and washing the combs for me, sweeping the floor. That was our bonding."

Murray was peering out the window of the barber shop

and he suddenly bolted for the door. "Mona, you're my savior, babe. The refrigeration man just pulled his truck in the alley. Will you just come talk to him a minute? You know the lingo."

Mona took the coffee cup out of Murray's hands. "Don't you worry, hon. We'll get this licked in time for the dinner shift. Sal, later." With that Mona led Murray across the street like he was an invalid. Murray waved pitifully back to Sal.

"On Thirty-ninth Street, it's never too easy," Sal said to the priest.

FIVE

CLOSE to on time, Heaven and the guys pulled up in front of the Aspen Resort Association, where a tent had been erected for participants of the festival to pick up their registration packets. As panel members, they were invited to a few extra events. European wine councils and California cheese makers and Costa Rican coffee roasters all wanted to impress the chefs and restaurant owners and food and wine writers that participated in the festival. They all tried doing that by hosting the best parties.

Chris and Joe pawed through their schedules. "Heaven, help us. You've been here before. You didn't tell us there were so many things to do every day. How do you decide between the 'Perfect Pie Crust' class and 'How to Cook a Whole Fish'?"

"Easy," Heaven said with a shrug. "I go to wine seminars. I already know a little about how to cook, but I always need more wine education. As panel members, you'll never get in the really big celebrities' classes, like Julia Child, anyway. We'll sit down this afternoon and go over it all."

"So where are you meeting Rowland and where is he taking you for lunch?" Joe asked, unable to stop pestering Heaven about the winemaker.

"Right here in front of the tent at one-thirty, which is almost now. And I have no idea where we'll go and I sure wouldn't tell you two if I did. You'd probably send champagne to our table or something totally dumb. Would you guys go up to the Hotel Jerome and poke around?''

"What are we looking for?" Chris asked eagerly, slipping into his detecting mode. The whole staff of Cafe Heaven had played amateur sleuths a couple of times, when disasters had threatened the restaurant and Heaven. Chris had a Columbo outfit, complete with rumpled raincoat, and a Rockford outfit: polyester sports jacket, sans-a-belt pants, and wide tie. Had he brought them in the prop case? he wondered.

"That's where our session will be held. Find out what room our workshop will be held in. See where the nearest bathrooms are, or if there might be a dressing room nearby. You know, just generally get the lay of the land," Heaven said.

"That's all?" Chris said, sounding disappointed with the mundane nature of the assignment.

"No problem," Joe piped in. "We'll introduce ourselves to the staff. But can we eat first? That breakfast burrito seems years ago."

"Main Street Bakery has a place to eat outside and an espresso machine. It's down a couple of blocks," Heaven pointed west, then turned and pointed in the opposite direction: "And there's designer pizzas at Mezzaluna. If you want cutting edge, most of those open just for dinner, but I've heard Ajax Tavern is good and open for lunch. The chef was nominated for Best Chef last year. It's over off Durant right by the Gondola lift. Do you have money?"

"Yes, yes. You gave us our per diems in Kansas City," Chris said.

Heaven smiled. "I wish they could be more. You're missing lots of shifts at the cafe. What I gave you won't make up for the lost tip money, I'm afraid. And this place is as expensive as . . ."

"New York City," the guys said in unison. "You told us. And I quote, 'How can rich people from New York think they're having fun if things don't cost too much?' We'll find the local hangouts in no time, trust us. Oh, lookie there. Here comes your date,'' Joe said, backing out of range as Heaven tried to give him a whack on the butt.

It was hard not to notice Rowland Alexander. First, he was at least six-foot-three. Then there were the piercing eyes, the gorgeous salt-and-pepper hair and matching beard, and the oozing charm. Rowland was a well-known winemaker from Australia who was credited with bringing Australian wines to the attention of the American wine-drinking public. Once a year Rowland toured the United States on behalf of all the Australian wineries, and that's how he and Heaven had met.

Holding his Kansas City wine dinner at Cafe Heaven wasn't his first choice. But the elegant, white-tablecloth restaurants hadn't been interested in Australian wines when Rowland started these tours. Heaven, however, already had four Australian wines on her list. Heaven's trendy-but-poor midtown customers were always looking for alternatives to those expensive California cabernets. When Rowland's wholesaler called and explained the situation, Heaven didn't mind being asked to do a dinner after the fancy establishments had said no. It turned out to be good for both Rowland and Heaven. That very first dinner matching food and Australian wines sold out. Now that Australian wines were accepted, even in the Midwest, Rowland still hosted his wine dinners at Cafe Heaven in Kansas City.

Chris and Joe greeted Rowland and made a quick exit, something that relieved Heaven to no end. She could see them grinning back at her, but at least they hadn't made a scene in front of Rowland who was bearing down on her, a big smile on his face. Everybody has a smile on their face, Heaven thought as she looked around at the excited foodies getting their registration packages. I guess it's my turn. Relax and enjoy yourself for a minute. You made it here in one piece. Everything is fine.

Rowland Alexander grabbed Heaven and scooped her

close. She fit perfectly in the crook of his arm. "Welcome! How was the trip?"

"I'm glad to report Kansas is still there, preventing the Rockies from falling in the Mississippi River."

Rowland laughed and put his hand on Heaven's elbow, gently leading her away from the line of registrants and toward the parking lot. "So that's what Kansas is for."

Just then Chris came barreling back around the corner. "I'm glad you're not gone. We didn't make plans for later. Do you want to pick us up?"

Rowland broke in. "Where are you staying? On the phone you said someone had loaned you their house."

Chris pointed up and north. "Up on the mountain somewhere behind a gate, if you please. The house is as big as the lodge at Yosemite Park."

Rowland looked at Heaven and glanced at his watch. "If Chris and Joe can find their way back to your lodge, I'll be glad to drive you home after lunch. We're meeting some other Aussies at Woody Creek, and we're late."

Heaven started digging in her purse for the car keys. "Can you find the way?"

Chris nodded. "I left a trail of bread crumbs. And the map is still in the car. We'll be home by three-thirty so you can get in."

Heaven handed over the keys and Chris gave a wave over his shoulder. Rowland steered her to a four-wheel-drive Jeep and they quickly sped west out of town, turning north on Cemetery Road.

"Wow, you know the shortcut to Woody Creek Tavern," Heaven said. "I'm impressed."

"I have been coming to this gig, as you would say, for six years now. Going to Woody Creek is a part of *The Real Dish* Festival as far as I'm concerned. How about you?"

"I've been to *The Real Dish* twice before. Lots of Kansas City people have houses in Aspen, so I can usually get a free place to stay. And one of my husbands . . ."

"Oh, oh. One? That implies there have been more than one. I should have known," Rowland said.

"And that, my dear, is another story. Sol Steinberg was a great skier. I must confess once I went to Woody Creek Tavern ten days in a row hoping to see Hunter Thompson in person."

"Oh, yes, the infamous journalist. Well, even without Hunter Thompson, I find Woody Creek full of local color. Good margaritas, too. When you're looking at three days of wine drinking, there's nothing like a base of tequila to start you off."

Rowland slowed down for the speed bump that announced they were almost at the log building that housed an art gallery, the Woody Creek post office, and the tavern. The whole complex was surrounded by trailers. "Here we are in the Rocky Mountains, in one of the prettiest towns in America, and we make a beeline for a honky-tonk in the middle of a trailer park."

"And we're proud to be here," Rowland said as he parked the car on the other side of the highway. As they walked across the narrow road, laughter erupted from the deck. A wood lattice fence created a place for tables, most of them the old hippie kind made out of cable spools with umbrellas sticking out of the hole in the middle. There were multi-colored plastic lanterns strung everywhere. A stuffed animal that looked something like a wild boar was nailed above the door. It had sunglasses perched crookedly on its glass eyes, the stunt of some drunk rock climber, no doubt. The front deck was full of winemakers, most of them from Australia or New Zealand from the sound of the accents.

Heaven and Rowland joined in and soon were downing margaritas, guacamole, and cheeseburgers with the best of them. After more than an hour of whooping, most of the others left to find their hotel rooms. Heaven and Rowland ordered some coffee and an apple dumpling.

"I love your friends," Heaven said as she looked at the

clutter of empty glasses around them. "They know how to have a good time."

"They're good mates, that's for sure," Rowland said with a smile.

Heaven was tickled at that term. Rowland usually spoke with an accent more British than Australian. She assumed he had been educated in England. But being around his "mates" had definitely brought out his native accent. "I love it when you talk like that." Heaven couldn't help flirting just a little. "But we should talk about business. Did you get the fax I sent you last week, laying out what we thought would work for our session and be mildly amusing?"

Rowland had just dug into the apple dumpling and looked up happily with his mouth full. He nodded yes and pointed up, as in wait just a minute, then took a sip of coffee. "As they say in the mother tongue, absolutely brilliant. It will be a smash hit, I know. They send someone from the magazine to every workshop and demonstration to introduce the panelists or the cook. I'll be there because I want to tell everyone why I asked you to do this particular workshop and then you three can do your thing. Usually everyone saves time for a question and answer session the last ten minutes or so. Have you been to any of the professional seminars before?"

Heaven nodded. "I always find one or two that sound good, like 'Employee Compensation Methods.'"

Rowland smiled. "I caught her 'How to Cook a Duck' the first year I was at the festival. She's a genius. I hope she'll be at the party tonight. You all got your invitations, didn't you?"

"Sure did. 'The Wines of Australia and New Zealand invite you to meet the Nominees for Best Chef of the Year.' Where are we going?"

Rowland laughed as he got up and threw money down on the tip tray containing their bill. "Surprise. I can't tell. But you did see the 'Bring a Jacket' part on the bottom of the invitation, didn't you? That's important so you won't freeze your tail off.''

"I promise we'll all wear jackets, but at least give me a hint," Heaven said as they walked across the road. She punched Rowland's arm playfully. He laughed and scooped her close again, like he had done when they had met earlier at the registration tent. Too close. As Rowland's arm brushed her breast, her nipple hardened. Heaven felt a blush coming on. ''Give me a rundown on the nominees,'' she said as she got in the car. Changing the subject seemed important.

Rowland looked over at her knowingly. Winemakers were notorious for the trouble they got into on the road. He didn't blame Heaven for sidestepping their attraction to each other, but he wasn't easily deterred. If not this year, maybe next year. ''OK. Five nominees again this year. There's that Cajun chef from somewhere around New Orleans.''

''Ernest Laveau from Houma, I bet.''

Rowland glanced over and nodded. ''Ernest. Yeah, that's it. Then there's Lola Castro from Miami. She's an older woman, was a kid in Cuba, the family fled to Miami with nothing and started a little barrio cafe when she was a teenager. Now they still have that little cafe in the barrio, but also a fancy, white-tablecloth restaurant over on Ocean Drive and one in Coconut Grove and a new one opening soon in Orlando. Great story.''

''Lola sounds like my kind of woman. Who else?''

''The biggest news is that Sergio La Sala is finally nominated and so is his son.''

Heaven snapped back to earth. She had been half listening and half daydreaming, looking out the window at the rushing water in the valley below. Now Rowland had 100 percent of her attention again. ''Tony La Sala is nominated for Best Chef? You've got to be kidding,'' Heaven said with something between irony and anger in her tone of voice.

''Why, do you know him? Is he a friend?''

''Well, I wouldn't go that far, but I did make the mistake of hiring him a couple of summers ago. He worked for me about six months. Seems Mr. La Sala was touring America trying to—and I quote—'break out of the straightjacket of my father's shadow.' No more Italian cooking for him, he said. He was going to find his own cuisine. He was an arrogant pain in the ass is what he was. The staff hated him. He was always dropping names of the famous cooks he knew through his father. He thought Kansas City was a hick town totally beneath him. And he didn't pull his weight in the kitchen and whined about what he did do. He was absolutely not worth the trouble. It was obvious at that time that he and his father weren't on good terms. Sergio phoned the cafe a couple of times but Tony wouldn't even talk to him.''

Rowland turned on to the highway and headed back into town. ''They still aren't on speaking terms,'' he said. ''Rumors say it's been two to five years since they've laid eyes on each other. Tony is the chef of a private club here in Aspen, the Cavern Club. I guess it's where the Hollywood stars hang.''

''That gets the second 'you've got to be kidding' of the day! Tony La Sala is a chef to the stars? I've heard of the Cavern Club and I thought it had a pretty good reputation. Well, either the stars have no taste buds or a miracle has happened, and Tony has learned to cook. I guess miracles are always a possibility.''

''Was he a bad cook?'' Rowland asked.

''Well, he wasn't a good cook, and he wouldn't listen to anyone, so I don't know how he could improve,'' Heaven answered. ''Back to Sergio. Tell me why you said he was *finally* nominated?''

''Sergio must be sixty years old by now. He wrote the definitive Italian cookbook thirty years ago. He's been a star since then, a San Francisco institution. Most of his peers were nominated for this award fifteen years ago, when the festival began.''

''Why has he been snubbed?''

''I don't know why, but I know by whom. Linda Lunch has been the editor of *The Real Dish* since the second year of the festival, fourteen years ago. Word has it there's bad blood between Sergio and Linda. No one knows why Linda, usually so eager to dish the dirt, won't tell. Neither will Sergio.''

''Does Linda control the nominations?''

Rowland made a left and headed past the post office and up the mountain. ''You'll have to start giving me directions soon.''

Heaven touched his hand on the steering wheel. ''You're doing great so far. Follow the road until the fork and take a left there. Then follow that until you come to the guard station. What about the nominations?''

''Well, an editorial panel chooses the nominees. They are writers from all over the country as well as *Real Dish* people, but I've been told that if it's someone that Linda doesn't want nominated, they won't be.''

''So she must have wanted Sergio on the slate this year,'' Heaven mused. ''Maybe she finally buried the hatchet.''

Rowland shook his head. ''Right in his back. Linda probably got reams of heat from people asking her why one of the country's greatest chefs had never even been nominated for her award. So she found a way to nominate him and his son at the same time. At the best, the two of them will have to be together, something they obviously don't enjoy. At the worst, one of them will beat the other.''

''Which will make the father feel like shit, no matter which one of them wins. This Linda Lunch must be a piece of work.''

''Oh, yeah. I can hardly wait to see you two in action together,'' Rowland said as he stopped at the gate and Heaven talked to a guard. She and Rowland signed a sheet and they pushed on.

''Who's the fifth nominee, not that they stand a chance with that lineup?''

''A barbecue cooker from Texas. He's got a real act, Wild West chuckwagon, the whole nine yards. Can't remember his name right now. He's Hispanic, I think.''

As the car pulled up in front of Peter Cooper's palace Heaven decided the festival was definitely getting interesting. She grinned as she opened the car door and said, "I take back what I said about the fifth nominee not standing a chance. Bo Morales is good."

Rowland yelled out the open window, "You know this guy?"

Heaven stopped at the door and blew a kiss in Rowland's direction. "Thanks for a great lunch." Then she was gone, leaving Rowland to his own vivid imagination.

SIX

CHRIS, Joe, and Heaven were lined up on a tapestry-covered couch the size of Akron, drinking Diet Cokes, looking out at the mountains and talking about their afternoons. Chris and Joe had reported on their trip to the Hotel Jerome and their exploration of the town. Heaven told them about lunch with the Aussies and the news that they would be seeing their friend Bo Morales at this event.

"So now you don't just have one guy who's sweet on you, you've got two," Joe said with that twinkle in his eye.

"I've always had good luck in Colorado. I used to come out here fairly often with one of my loved ones," Heaven said.

"Which husband did you come out here skiing with?"

"Guess," Heaven teased.

Chris and Joe huddled down in the cushions. This was fun. "Husband number one was Sandy Martin. Lawyers generally like to ski, but Sandy just doesn't look the type," Joe said.

Heaven nodded. "You mean the three Bs? Big, brawny, and bearded? You're right. Sandy likes to get off the ground, but it's to fly his airplane. That's one of those secrets people don't know about us prairie folks. We all love flying. When I was growing up in Kansas, so many of our neighbors had their own small planes. My folks had a friend who owned four or five department stores in several little Kansas towns. Of course, I didn't know they were little towns then. They seemed like big towns to me. Anyway, this guy used his plane to fly to each of his stores one day a week. Sandy's dad is a rancher, you know. He had a plane and Sandy bought his father's old plane when he bought a new one about twenty years ago. He's been flying ever since. His dad still flies too.''

Chris liked hearing Heaven's history with Sandy Martin. They had met a couple of years before when Sandy's date dropped dead in Cafe Heaven. "Are Sandy's parents still alive?" he asked.

"Oh my, yes. I try to see them when I go out to have the family business meetings with my brother. They're in their late seventies. Sandy's brother runs the ranch, but the Martins are still going strong. Did I ever tell you about our wedding?"

"Tell."

"It was at the Martins' ranch. Really, it was my dream wedding, the best one ever.''

"Do you think that's because it was the first one?"

"Oh, no. This really was the best wedding. Picture this ranch in Kansas in early June when everything is still pretty and green, not like August when everything is burned up and brown with the heat. The wedding ceremony was out on an Indian burial mound in Flint Hills. There was a sweet little stone church that the Martins had restored. Everyone had to ride a horse or in a horse-driven buggy to get to the church. The Martins had a wonderful collection of buggies, wagons, and carriages. Sandy and I had finished our first year at Kansas State in Manhattan. I guess we were nineteen and very smitten with each other. Oh, I forgot one of the best parts. There was a Suzuki violin teacher in Council Grove, so we had about a hundred little kids playing Bach on their violins. It was spectacular. And they had a big barbecue pit and we had all kinds of grilled and barbecued meats, including buffalo burgers. The Martins had a herd of buffalos.''

"Were the ranchers and farmers enemies like in *Oklahoma*?" Joe asked.

"Not really. The Flint Hills aren't farm land. We lived north of Council Grove, where the farm land begins and Sandy's folks lived south of Council Grove, where the Flint Hills start. And my folks were just great. Everyone loved my folks."

"You still miss them, don't you?"

"Sure. They died the next year in that awful car accident. I was just twenty. I'm still always thinking of things I want to tell them." Heaven gazed out the window at the mountains ahead. "And they never got to meet their wonderful grand-daughter."

Chris laughed. "I have a feeling Iris's father isn't the ski nut."

"You're right about that. Rock-and-roll stars don't like to stay outside that much. And we weren't married long enough to make it to a ski season."

"How long were you Mrs. McGuinne?" Joe asked, trying to keep it all straight.

"We got married in December and divorced the next fall. I guess we could have made it to Switzerland to ski, but we went to Monaco to play in the casinos instead. Dennis won big, as I recall. I did too. I got pregnant with Iris."

"Do you miss Iris since she's been at school in England?" Chris asked.

"Yeah, but it's been great for her and her father to spend time together. Dennis has really straightened out his life."

Chris was still playing the guessing game. "Let's see, Sandy, then Dennis, then Ian Wolff. Was it Ian Wolff who liked to ski?"

Heaven shook her head. "Painters aren't usually fond of the outdoors either, unless they're landscape painters, of course."

"I know I've heard you say Ian Wolff was the love of your life. You miss him too, don't you?"

"Every day," Heaven said in a silly accent, but she was visibly uncomfortable. "Let's move on."

Chris and Joe exchanged knowing looks. "Well, I know Jason Kelley and he likes to go to the beach in the winter, not the mountains. It must be the guy who owned the uniform company," Joe said.

"Right you are. Sol Steinberg. He was a wonderful skier, among other things. He was just one terrific person," Heaven said with a catch in her voice. She abruptly got up and went over to their registration material. Chris and Joe could tell the history lesson was over. They didn't press the issue and dutifully went over to the table and took a seat. Heaven opened up a thick program. "This has all the seminars listed plus the speakers' bios."

"Does it have us?" Chris asked, always thinking of his press clips.

Heaven nodded. "But it only has a picture of me. I'm sorry for hogging the bio," she said as she flipped to a page full of mug shots.

"Well, at least read it to us," Joe said.

"Heaven Lee is the chef-owner of an eclectic world food bistro, Cafe Heaven, in Kansas City, Missouri, that has been featured in *The Real Dish* and many other national publications. The wine list of Cafe Heaven has been the subject of numerous awards and articles and she and her staff will share the secrets of how they sell lesser-known varietals as well as other wine-selling tips in their theatrical presentation, 'How Not to Sell Wine,'" Heaven recited.

"Oh, dear, I hope we can pull this off," Joe said solemnly.

Heaven gave him a little hug. "We know what we're doing, sweetie. Or we will know what we're doing by the time Saturday morning comes around. Speaking of that," she said, "I'm calling a rehearsal for tomorrow."

"The drill sergeant has called a rehearsal," Chris teased.

Heaven hit him with the program. "Don't be cute. You know what I mean. As the boss I am calling a rehearsal, little mister. In the meantime, we all have to be thinking of ways to act out these scenes we wrote. Like how are we going to pull off the one about making people beg to see the wine list? Let's not talk about it anymore now. Sleep on it. Tomorrow our creativity will flow.''

Joe was giving Chris a look that said shut up before you get us in trouble. He could see that Chris thought he should be the director of this little show. ''We're on it. We'll let the id take it awhile. So, tell us what happens at this food and wine fest.'' Joe could be diplomatic sometimes.

''Well, tonight,'' Heaven said, ''we get to go to a party not open to the public. It's sponsored by Wines of Australia and New Zealand and it's to introduce the Best Chef nominees to the press and the panel members.''

''Where's the party?'' Joe asked.

''I don't know. Rowland said it was a surprise and I couldn't wriggle the truth out of him.''

Both Chris and Joe opened their mouths to make a smart crack, but thought better of it. The two men studied the program carefully, trying to avoid the eye contact that would make them giggle like sixth graders. ''What is this Grand Tasting that happens twice a day?''

''It's a veritable orgy, but not of sex or food. Waggoner Park is in the middle of Aspen and is covered with tents. Twice a day, all these wineries and importers pour wine. You pick up a glass at the door and then you just drink for an hour or so. Needless to say, all the free wine your very expensive ticket can provide is one of the reasons this event is so popular with the winos.''

Joe's eyes were large with the possibilities Heaven had just hinted at. ''I'm impressed. I would expect no less out of Aspen. It's the pinnacle of tasteful excess.''

Chris was pacing and flipping through the program notes. ''So tomorrow we can choose between Barbara Tropp doing Chinese and Patricia Wells doing French Provencal, then move along to Sergio doing Italian or a wine tasting about Pinot Noir? It's like a treasure trove.''

Heaven nodded. ''You have the general idea. Great teachers and lots of booze. Five thousand people are totally gone on wine and food and high altitudes. Luckily most people can walk to their hotels. Unfortunately, not us. And the Aspen police are very strict. If we get separated and you need to come home and you're feeling the wine, call a cab. Another thing about Aspen, everything is printed in one of the two free newspapers. All arrests, even if it's a famous person. There's a saying, something about if you don't want to see it in print, don't let it happen."

"So this is how Aspen keeps all the star egos in check. Fear of the local press," Joe said.

Heaven grabbed the program out of Chris's hand. "I'm demanding full attention for the biggest news of the day."

Chris and Joe threw themselves on a couch and looked up expectantly, afraid to make a peep.

"Guess what scumbag is up for Best Chef?" She paused. "That horrible Tony La Sala who worked at the cafe. Can you believe it? He could barely make stock and now he's going to be famous. Life is not fair."

"Heaven, are you mad that you didn't get nominated?" Joe asked.

"Of course not," Heaven said too quickly. "But for Sergio La Sala it must be horrible. He hasn't been nominated before and he really deserves it and now he and his no-good son are running against each other. Rowland says that the editor of *The Real Dish* has it in for Sergio."

Chris's face lit up. "I bet Tony will be at the party tonight. I can hardly wait to get my hands on him. He deliberately lost my food order for a party of eight on a busy Friday night. And then had nerve enough to smirk about it."

Heaven got up, shaking her head. "And you're still pissed about it two years later. Remind me never to get on your bad side. Let's get ready. We have to leave here in an hour, at six."

Joe raised his hand like a third grader. "Wait, what happens with this Best Chef thing?"

"Saturday night, the first five hundred people who sent in

their checks for the festival get to come to a dinner that all the nominees cook.''

"We get to vote?'' Chris asked.

"No, only the five hundred get to vote. But we get to eat the food and make our own judgments. It's a blast. That's Saturday night. Sunday at noon there will be this big soiree on Aspen Mountain.''

"How do we get up there?'' Chris asked anxiously. He wasn't fond of heights and had even felt a little light-headed along the interstate when they climbed into the mountains from Denver.

"In the ski gondolas, silly,'' Heaven replied. "They have chamber music groups and champagne. Then they announce the Best Chef award. Monday, we go home. We now have fifty minutes to get beautiful. Lecture is officially over. There will, however, be a test later.''

SEVEN

FOR a moment, Tab Garner gave up. I'm calling everything off, he thought. He sat down on the edge of the bed and started taking off his shoes. He looked in the mirror on the other side of the room and started talking to himself aloud. "It is inhuman to force a Mississippi native to endure what passes for summer in these mountains. I'll freeze at this damn outdoor party tonight, if I don't die from exhaustion first."

Tab continued to talk and get undressed. "Linda would skin me alive if I took to the bed. She has more energy than five normal souls. She would not be amused. Not that I have to worry about what she thinks much longer."

Tab chose a new outfit, soft denim work shirt, vintage tie, Gap khakis, and cowboy boots, and smiled at his image in the mirror. He put a perfect knot in his tie and slipped on a navy cashmere sweater that he had picked up at the shop, Cashmere Aspen, in the afternoon. "Hello, there. You look like the new art director of *Foodies*. You handsome devil. I hear when you left *The Real Dish*, Linda Lunch actually cried and begged you to stay." Tab Garner chuckled at his reflection one more time, tossed his head with approval at what he saw, and turned out the light.

The Hotel Jerome was headquarters for all the magazine staff. He moved quickly down the stairs to avoid the elevators. Tab would know everyone on the elevator and before long someone would want to walk with him over to the Little Nell, which was on the other side of Main Street from the Jerome and up the hill near the ski lifts. Right now he couldn't afford company. As he passed through the lobby, one of the desk clerks called his name.

"Mr. Garner, I have a note here for you."

Linda Lunch took the cucumbers off her closed eyelids. Next year she'd have to put on a seminar about the benefits of applying food on the outside of your body, including sea-weed wraps, papaya facials, and oatmeal rubs.

Linda got up and looked carefully at the outfit she had pulled together before her rest. She had laid out skinny black leather pants, black silk camisole, skinny little black cashmere short-sleeved sweater, black leather Fendi jacket. She took a Donna Karan top out of her closet and held it up to her slight frame. Maybe this would be better than the cashmere. Her hands were shaking slightly. She glanced up at the mirror and her trembling finger traced the outline of a faint bruise on her stomach. Another yellowish splotch was on her upper arm near the shoulder. Linda looked away quickly.

She was floored by the realization she was nervous. She hadn't been nervous since she forced the hand of the next-to-last publisher five years ago. He had folded in the standoff and resigned. Linda remembered it had been about her expensive tour of all the three-star restaurants in France. What had his name been, anyhow?

Linda threw the Donna Karan on the bed and started plucking her already barely noticeable eyebrows. Everything at the festival so far had gone fine. All but a couple of the panel members were in town and those two were due to be picked up later in the evening at the airport. The wineries and importers had all checked in. No shipments of wine had been lost. No one was furious about their placement in the tasting tent. And all the chefs were here, waiting to be introduced for the first time tonight. Of course, scads of people already knew who the nominees were. After all, you had to print bios and programs and coordinate the menu, so lots of people knew. But the public wouldn't until tonight. Not that the actual public would be at the Aussies' party, but the staff and winemakers and presenters were as close to the public as Linda ever went. Tomorrow the consumers would find out who was up for Best Chef.

Linda slipped into the leather pants, lying back on the bed to zip them up. She wasn't sure she was really up to this. Personal feelings were one thing that Linda Lunch had no patience for. But it was time. She had put off dealing with this as long as any self-respecting, self-absorbed career woman with a house in Sag Harbor and a Jaguar in New York City she never drove, could put off something, which was years.

Tonight she would put part two of her diabolical little plan in motion. Now, what shade lipstick was right?

Tab Garner looked around in the dim light of the Little Nell's hotel bar. He had dodged all the *Real Dish* staff members who were milling around outside. How dare they change the pick up place to the hotel where he was trying to have a secret meeting?

Tab ordered a beer at the bar and sat at a small table in the shadows. Suddenly, a man sat down across from him. He looked like many of the local Aspen residents, long hair pulled back in a ponytail, perfectly rumpled denim work shirt, fishing vest, jeans, hiking boots. He stared at Tab with interest. "Hey, Tab. How do you like Aspen so far?"

Tab took a drink of his beer and gazed around. "Funny, you don't look like the publisher of *Foodies* magazine. I was supposed to meet him here."

The man pulled his chair over to Tab's table. "After that little incident last year, when you found the assistant editor of *Wine Geek* magazine dead drunk in the tasting tent and you put him on a plane to Denver before he sobered up, other food magazine folks think it best to avoid Aspen at this time of year.''

Tab chuckled. ''That was fun, depositing the world's foremost expert on Burgundy on a small plane in a heap, as he babbled about Zinfandel. I bet he was sick as a dog on takeoff. I must admit I'll miss Aspen in June. This year is bittersweet for me.''

The other man looked at Tab with disgust. ''You'll get over it. After all, with the big bucks you'll be pulling down at your new gig you can come to Aspen whenever you want. Now, your new employers have asked me to do a few little jobs for them this week and you know what, Tab, old buddy, they have volunteered you to help me. Wasn't that nice of them?''

Tab shifted uncomfortably. ''I don't have time. . . .''

The man put his hand on Tab's arm and squeezed hard. ''This is not an option, you little fag. Now shut up and drink your beer. I'll lay this out for you real fast.'' He slid a medicine bottle half full of liquid in Tab's direction.

''You're driving too fast! This road is dangerous!''

Linda Lunch looked over at Sergio La Sala and gave a short laugh, one without mirth. The four-wheel-drive wagon she was piloting was precariously close to the edge of the road and there was no guardrail. The drop was considerable, even by Colorado standards. To make matters worse, a large truck was coming down the mountain toward them.

''After all these years, Sergio, surely you trust me.'' Just to emphasize the point, Linda swerved the van slightly toward the truck. Sergio grabbed on to the dashboard, white-knuckled.

''Cut this shit out, I'm too old to die on some mountain road with you. I agreed to ride up to this barbecue bullshit with you because you said it was important. Was that just a ploy to kill me?''

Linda slowed down as they got to a particularly tricky group of hairpin turns. ''Just think, Sergie. I've kept my mouth shut for, what is it, thirty years now? Doesn't that give me some credence in your book?"

Sergio relaxed slightly. "It goes both ways, Linda. If you had opened your mouth, I'm not the only one who would be hurt by it. You're the one who would look worse."

"Well, Sergie, that's what I wanted to tell you today. I'm ready to risk that. Now is the time. This weekend."

"No."

Sergio and Linda drove the rest of the way to the party in silence. Several times Sergio had started to argue, then stopped. Linda drove carefully the rest of the way, waiting for Sergio to say something more than no. Finally they arrived at their destination. Linda looked over at Sergio with a smirk on her face. "Cat got your tongue?"

"Linda, I'm not going to let you do this."

Linda opened the door of the Jeep and hopped out. "Well, Sergie honey, just try and stop me."

EIGHT

"IT'S a bird. Well, a dead bird now," Mona yelled down at Murray from the roof of Cafe Heaven.

"A bird?" Murray repeated.

"It happens, Murray. A bird flew into the gizmo up here and caused the breaker to flip the power off. The cooling fella has run to get this one little part that got bent."

"Gizmo? Bent part? Mona, are you telling me the whole story?" Murray felt like such a coward for not going up on the roof himself, but heights had never been his strong suit. "And Mona, what was a bird doing flying around on our roof in the middle of the night?"

"Murray, you're getting on my last nerve. I know about cats, not birds. The point is everything will be hunky-dory soon, and it won't cost an arm and a leg, just a leg." Mona chuckled at her own joke and fanned the air with her hands. "It sure is hot as blazes up here."

Sal, who had been watching the proceedings from across the street had finally come over to make sure everything was OK. "Then why the heck don't you climb down from up there? I'll hold the ladder."

Mona waved gaily down at them, happy to be braver than the men. Brian and Pauline had watched the whole thing, but now wandered back in the kitchen. If the air conditioning was coming on soon, they'd start prepping for dinner. It might not be chilly inside the restaurant tonight but at least it wouldn't be unbearable.

"I'll be down in a minute," Mona said. "I can see a piece of tar paper or something wrapped around the air conditioner on my roof. I'll just go over and get rid of it. It can't be good for the motor," she said like the daughter of an air conditioning man that she was.

"No," Sal and Murray yelled more or less at the same time.

"Don't be crazy," Sal said sternly.

"You'll have a heatstroke up there," Murray added.

Mona looked down at them scornfully. "I'll be down in a sec."

"The roof isn't the same height," Murray argued.

"Yeah, it's all of six inches different. Just watch, guys. Everything will be just fine." With that, Mona walked over to the roof of her shop, which was flush against the restaurant roof but slightly lower. She waved down again and threw a leg over onto the roof of her shop.

"See," she exclaimed smugly as she threw the second leg over and the rest of her body after it. Suddenly Mona disappeared completely from sight. An "Oh my God," trailing off the roof into the hot summer air was all that seemed to be left of her.

Sal and Murray both started yelling. "Mona, where the hell are you? Brian, come out here quick. Mona!"

All of a sudden, Mona's gray head appeared over the lip of the roof. "It's all right," she said in a very shaky voice.

"What happened?" Murray asked hysterically. "Brian, call 911."

"There was a hole and my leg got caught when I stepped down." She laughed weakly. "My landlord must have hired the cheapest roofers in town."

"But you're OK now?" Sal asked in his no-nonsense, tell-me-the-truth voice. By this time, a small crowd had gathered: Brian and Pauline and Robbie and two or three folks from off the street, and the air conditioner man, back with the new part.

"Just fine, except for one thing." There was an expectant silence. "My leg seems to be caught. I can't get it out."

NINE

THE bus was slowly filling up. Slowly because every one had to stop and say hello to someone. Joe and Heaven slipped in the seats toward the back. Chris sat in the aisle seat opposite. For a minute. All of a sudden, he practically leapt to the window seat, smiling coquettishly down the length of the vehicle.

"Chris, what in the world?" Heaven looked over and saw him actually fluffing his hair. Chris had flaxen hair, which fell almost to his shoulders. It was his pride and joy. Heaven was sure Snyder was just some Ellis Island shorthand for a Swedish or Finnish name that his great grandfather came to America with. Heaven followed Chris's eye and saw what had caught his attention. Another cute blond was headed their way. This one had a Brooks Brothers haircut and muscles that showed some serious gym time. He also had a great smile and seemed to know people in every row. The seat by Chris was the first empty one. Now Heaven understood why Chris had moved.

The very next moment, Mr. Muscles plopped down beside Chris and stuck out his hand. "I think you're the first person I don't already know on this damn bus. You can leave New York, but not by coming to Aspen. Tab Garner. I work for *The Real Dish* in an editorial capacity. Actually, I try to keep our fearless leader, Linda Lunch, from snatching someone bald. Who are you, handsome?''

Chris looked across the aisle like a cat with a canary. Joe and Heaven were watching every move. ''I'm Chris Snyder. Is that a Southern accent I hear?''

All of a sudden, the bus lurched forward and headed east out of town.

Before the bus reached full speed, Chris and Tab were chatting like old friends.

Heaven looked out at the road. ''We're going up in the direction of Independence Pass. No wonder we're in mini-buses.''

''Why?'' Joe asked, looking out at the vistas.

''You wouldn't want to be in a full-sized bus on this road. It would be terrifying. This part of the highway is so narrow and steep, it's only open a few months in the summer. In the winter, Aspen is like a giant cul-de-sac, one way in, one way out.'' Heaven glanced across the aisle. ''What do you think?''

''About?'' Joe asked, continuing to stare out the window.

''About Chris and this gorgeous guy. They seem to be getting along, don't they?''

Joe clucked at her and shook a finger in her direction. ''You sound like some matchmaking aunt. Chris always says he isn't interested in having a relationship at this time in his life.''

Heaven said defensively, ''I know, I know. But a little flirtation couldn't hurt, could it?''

Joe patted her knee. ''Flirtations aren't what they used to be, before HIV.''

''You can say that again,'' Heaven retorted. ''Now they really are just flirtations. I hate the nineties.''

All of a sudden, Harlin Garner, aka Tab, turned his attention across the aisle toward Heaven. ''You can sure say that again. The nineties have been a drag. I can hardly wait for that dad-blame millennium. I'm Tab Garner. I work for *The Real Dish*. And I just found out that you're Heaven Lee.

Your restaurant is one of my favorite places that I've never been.''

Heaven grinned. ''What a way with words. Have you even been to Kansas City?''

Tab shook his head. ''I try not to leave New York City too much. I might learn to love trees and clean air again. 'Course you never know what's around the next corner, do you?'' He turned and smiled at Chris, and they resumed talking animatedly.

''Whoa,'' Joe murmured to Heaven. ''I better pull Chris's chain a little. Trade seats with me.''

Heaven did as Joe asked and saw the look of terror on Chris's face. It wasn't that Joe was cuter or smarter than Chris. Chris could hold his own on that score. But Joe was notorious for making up ridiculous stories whenever any of his friends started flirting with someone new. The last time he sat down at a table with Chris and a new guy, he asked about Chris's wife and his twins. That potential new boyfriend had flown away faster than an owl after a field mouse.

Just knowing that his move to the aisle had given his buddy a start seemed to be enough for Joe this time. He introduced himself and asked Tab a perfectly reasonable question about his job. Heaven relaxed and daydreamed. They were climbing to well over ten thousand feet. The road had lots of hairpin curves and though she wouldn't admit it to anyone, the turns could get to her when she wasn't driving. She focused on the back of the seat in front of her. Just when her stomach started doing flips, the bus rounded a bend and there was Independence Homestead, one of the famous ghost towns that surrounded Aspen.

Today it had been invaded by a decidedly live team of modern humans with a party on their minds. There were two huge tents, a bluegrass fiddler was playing, and Bo Morales had set up his chuckwagon, complete with mule team. Guests were already wandering around, reading historical signs and poking their heads in old miners' shacks, looking like ants against the vast mountainous background. Heaven could see

Rowland greeting the passengers rolling off another bus.

Tab Garner stood up and stretched nonchalantly like a cat.
"Let the games begin," he said with a big smile. "Heaven,
I can hardly wait to introduce you to my boss."

At that very moment, Linda Lunch appeared beside their
bus, peering in with an anxious look on her face. When she
spotted Tab, the look changed to impatience. Get the hell out
here, she mouthed silently. Her arms were waving wildly.

"I hope nothing's wrong," Heaven said with concern.
"Your boss looks upset."

Tab bowed to Heaven, indicating she should walk down
the aisle in front of him. "Nonsense. That's her in a calm
and contemplative mood. She's just bent out of shape because she expected me to be here when she arrived. But I
had a little business of my own to attend to." Tab laughed,
a laugh rich with undertones. "The idea that I might have a
life has never crossed her mind. Well, y'all, this was a pleasure. Chris, I'm countin' on you to rescue me from her in
fifty minutes. Deal?"

They all stepped off the bus and the editor swooped toward them. Chris nodded nervously. "Deal."

Tab broke away from their little group and was gone,
pulled toward the food tent by his fearless leader.

Chris looked after them with mixed feelings. "I hope she
won't hurt me when I try to rescue Tab."

Joe saw an opening and went for it like a slippery quar-
terback. "Yes, but can you say the same for Tab hurting
you? Oh, please, Tab. No, no, Tab."

Chris was not amused.

Heaven broke in. "OK. OK. Time out. Joe has been jerk-
ing your chain since Tab sat down next to you, and he was
stuck sitting with me. Let's drop it. Joe, behave. Chris, have
fun with your new friend. He seems nice, and he has a great
accent."

"Did you know Bo was going to cook tonight?" Chris
asked.

"No, I told you I couldn't get a thing out of Rowland

about this party. He wanted it to be a surprise. I didn't even know where we were going. At least now we know the food will be good. I was afraid we might have to eat Vegemite, or whatever that stuff is they like in Australia. I'm going to say hi to Bo. Do *not* follow me.''

Heaven looked around. It was an eerie, starkly beautiful place. The words ghost town had never seemed more appropriate. In the 1890s Independence Homestead was the first stop for miners coming across the mountain from the East looking for silver. The air was thin but invigorating. There was an electric current around the place that was undeniable. Heaven was sure this time it did not come from the boisterous food and wine revelers, but from the energy of the place itself.

Bo Morales had set up his portable pits down and away from the road and the tents, near a raging stream. Heaven heard a distant waterfall. Weathered wood houses, long abandoned, dotted the site. She stopped and touched the worn siding of one of the small shacks, wondering what the building had seen over the years.

''What would bring a person to such a wild place?'' Bo Morales asked as he appeared in front of Heaven, holding the most beautiful columbine she had ever seen. He offered it to her with a courtly bow.

Heaven laughed and took the flower. ''Not a damn highway, that's for sure.'' She slipped her arm in his. ''Last time I saw you, you stole flowers from a funeral arrangement. This time you probably broke some federal law, picking a wildflower. What's next?''

Bo tried to look sheepish. ''I promise to make a contribution to the conservation society. What a pleasant surprise, Heaven. I had no idea you would be here. Believe me, I'm glad to see a friendly face.''

Heaven took in Bo's appearance. Over the months since they first met, she had tried to persuade herself he wasn't as spectacular as she remembered him. Wistfully now, she admitted she hadn't made him more magnificent in her memory than he was in person. Bo had glossy black hair caught at the nape of his neck in a ponytail. His olive skin didn't prepare you for the beautiful blue eyes like the ones that made Paul Newman a legend. Then he smiled, and Heaven almost had to turn her head. Bo wanted to be a movie star some day. Heaven could imagine the voltage of that smile and those eyes on the big screen. She gave him what she hoped passed for a sisterly hug, and they headed for the chuckwagon.

"What's the matter?" she asked. "Have the foodies been mean to you?"

Bo shook his head. "No, of course not. Everyone has been very nice. And it was great of the Australians to ask me to cook for this party. Getting to make a little money will help with the expense of coming to Aspen. You know, each nominee has to pay for most of their own supplies and all the food for the big dinner. Feeding six or seven hundred people isn't cheap."

"I can certainly understand that. You have to spend a fortune to get famous in the food world. How did you get the wagon and the team here?"

"Horse trailers and a flatbed truck, just like always. That's another expense the other chefs don't have. Why, I bet that Cajun guy just threw some crayfish in a cooler and hopped on the jet."

"Yeah, and Tony La Sala just walked across Aspen, the idiot."

"Heaven, what do you know about Tony La Sala? Spill the beans, honey. But help me turn these ribs while we're talking. We need to feed these people before it gets too dark and cold up here. The first buses come back to get you all at nine."

Heaven grabbed a spare apron hanging on a hook on the back of the chuckwagon. "I'll be your sous chef any time and if you're sweet, I'll give you all the scoop we've collected so far." With that, the two went to work.

It was just a little after seven-thirty when Heaven, Bo, and all his helpers rang the dinner bell. The food tent had been set up so diners could go down both sides of the serving table. Tables and chairs filled the rest of the tent as well as the adjoining bar tent. Festival volunteers were busy tying back the tent flaps separating the two large tents to form one big room. There were portable heaters at all four corners making it very comfortable.

Rowland and his wine association had been marketing their wines as ones that went with any cuisine. So instead of trying to do a strictly Australian dinner, they had chosen slow-cooked, smoky meats to show off the variety of wonderful reds produced. There had been Yalumba, a well-made sparkling wine, and a variety of Chardonnays and Rieslings before dinner. The New Zealand contingent weighed in with their famous Sauvignon Blancs.

Bo wowed them. Down at the end of the table, there was a mother and daughter team, making fresh tortillas by hand on a fifty-gallon drum that was rigged as a brazier. There were pork ribs, goat meat called cabrito, quails, pork shoulders, and beef brisket, all arranged on huge tin platters. There were Bo's famous beans in a big blue splatter pot hanging on a tripod; he had won the Texas bean-cooking championship five times. There was coleslaw, carrot salad, pickled peaches. There were beaten biscuits and cornbread with cracklings, crispy bits of fried fat and skin in it. Bo had authentic quilt tops that he used as tablecloths and Western mementos, spurs, branding irons, and the like decorated the table.

Bo's Beans

1 lb. northern beans or other white beans
⅓ cup each yellow mustard and coarse ground spicy mustard
⅔ cup ketchup
⅔ cup bread crumbs
½ cup each brown sugar and molasses
1 T. apple cider vinegar

1 tsp. Louisiana hot sauce, such as Tabasco
1 tsp. soy sauce
1 dried ancho chili, soaked in water for twenty minutes
Options: ½ lb. hot country-style sausage, crumbled and browned or the burnt ends of your barbecue, such as brisket or pork shoulder. Bo would throw these little crispy bits of meat in the beans. If you have any such thing around when you make these beans, know it will be good in them.

Sort the dried beans, looking for rocks or other foreign material. Soak in a three-to-one ratio of water to beans overnight or at least three hours. Some people proceed on the theory that if you drain this soaking liquid you can prevent gas by removing indigestible sugar in the water. Others contend you lose valuable nutrients by draining the soaking water. Either way you will need to replace the water absorbed by the beans back to a three-to-one ratio. Bring beans to a boil but immediately reduce heat to a simmer. Cook until several test beans are just barely tender. Salt and other acids toughen the outer wall of the bean and extend cooking time so salt the beans to taste after this step.

If you are going to continue this recipe the next day, drain the beans and store them and their cooking liquid separately; that way they won't continue to cook in the hot broth. This will make it easier to cool the beans by rinsing them in cool water.

When you are ready to bake the beans, make sure you have enough broth to cover them. Add chicken stock or vegetable broth if you don't. Then add all the above ingredients, sticking the chili in the bean mixture whole. Top with the bread crumbs and bake 1 hour at 350 degrees or until the top is brown and the mixture is bubbling. Remember to remove the chili before serving.

Heaven gave Bo a peck on the cheek. "From one caterer to another, you do good work." Heaven knew he made most of his income doing big bashes like this. "You stand here and collect the kudos. I'm starved and I'm going to get a plate and find Chris and Joe. I've left them alone much too long. Either they're in big trouble or by now they've been asked to run the festival next year."

Bo kissed her hand, then laughed and tossed his head back. Heaven had seen him do this before and it was very disconcerting. "Thanks for the help and the information on my fellow candidates. When can I see you again? I have a fire-building demo tomorrow at three but other than that, I'm free. I'm staying at the Ritz."

"I'll leave a message tomorrow, I promise, and I'll see you before I leave tonight," Heaven said as she headed for the back of the food line. There were about one hundred and twenty or thirty guests. With two lines, Heaven knew it wouldn't take any time at all to get them fed. As she took her place she looked around for her friends and suddenly she realized she was standing right behind Linda Lunch herself. Heaven was curious about Linda after meeting Tab. She took a deep breath and ...

"Well, well, look who's here. Kansas City's prize chef," the scrawny editor gushed halfheartedly.

"Linda, I'm Heaven Lee. I'm so glad to meet you. I was so surprised and pleased to see my friend Bo Morales here in Aspen."

Linda looked her up and down with the expertise of a Nebraska meat inspector. "Friend, eh? Aren't you a little old for him?"

Heaven smiled beatifically. "Actually, Linda, Bo's a little old for me. Hank, the physician I'm involved with, is twenty-six."

Linda had to give her that one. "Touché, Heaven."

Heaven pressed on. "Bo and I met last year when he came to Kansas City for the World Series of Barbecue. By the way, Linda, that's an event your subscribers would probably love to read about."

"Probably," Linda said with little enthusiasm. "Maybe you can tell me what all this shit with the chuckwagon is about. I thought these barbecue cookers used big iron smokers or an entire Winnebago or some such crap."

Heaven came back with an insincere but hearty laugh that she hoped conveyed, Linda, how dumb can you get? "No, Linda, the teams, the people, usually sleep in the Winnebagos, not cook in them. You know, slow cooking is a twenty-four-hour-a-day-job. The meat needs constant attention. But chuckwagons, that's a whole subgenre of slow cooking, mostly in Texas and Oklahoma. They compete with authentic 1890's equipment. They use tin-lined ice coolers, no plastic containers, no foil or plastic wrap. They dig pits and bury the food in the ashes. They dress in turn-of-the-century clothes and their chuckwagons have to be functioning chuckwagons with authentic parts. If there's a coffee grinder, it has to be a working coffee grinder from the period. Bo told me he once got points taken off because a judge spotted a Diet Coke can in his wagon."

Linda shook her head, seemingly unimpressed. "Some people must be easily entertained or have too much time on their hands."

Suddenly, there was a loud crash from the buffet table. Linda Lunch looked over in the direction of the noise and started cursing softly. As she made a beeline for the commotion, Heaven instinctively followed her. Loud voices had taken up where the sound of broken glass left off. Now that Linda, with Heaven in her wake, had plowed through the crowd, they could both see the scene of the crime. Sergio La Sala was sitting very still, not moving a muscle. His head, back, and chair were covered with the contents of someone's overloaded plate. Ribs, baked beans, barbecue sauce, every red, sticky thing known to a cookout were stuck all over Sergio. A glass of red wine was broken and lying on its side, the contents dribbling off the table onto Sergio's lap.

And standing behind his father's chair, looking like a ten-year-old brat who had just pulled a fast one, was Tony La Sala. Heaven arrived just in time to hear Tony's smirking apology.

"Gosh, Dad. Long time, no see. I guess I was so overcome by the sight of my father, I lost my grip on the plate, there. Sorry about the mess."

With that, Tony, to the abject horror of Sergio's table of supporters, started to walk away. Everyone began yelling at once. Then, with the agility of someone half his age, Sergio twisted out of his chair, letting it fall over as he jumped up. He caught Tony by the back of his sweater, and twisted the material into a noose around his son's neck. He stepped close and spoke softly in his ear. He was whispering in Italian.

Damn, Heaven said to herself. Another reason I should know how to speak Italian. But Sergio quickly reverted to English.

"Son, you think you can get by with humiliating the old man, do you? Well, think again, bigshot. Think again!"

By this time Tony La Sala was gasping for breath and grabbing frantically at his father's hands. Almost immediately, several bystanders intervened. Heaven was surprised that one of them was Linda Lunch. She looked more like the type who would love to watch a good bloodletting.

Linda savagely pushed the two away from each other. "Listen, you motherfuckers," Linda said in a tone that brought silence to the whole tent, "if you two pull anything that will fuck up my festival, you will be sorrier than you ever imagined possible. Tony, I'll make sure you won't be able to get a job peeling onions. Sergie, your restaurant will be named Linda's after I get done with you. Do I make myself fucking crystal clear? Tab!" she screamed at the top of her lungs. Tab, of course, had found his way to the front of the crowd and was right by her side, waiting for orders with an expectant look. "Please see to it Sergio gets cleaned up and have someone drive him to the hotel. And tell that idiot Tony to stay clear of me the rest of the festival!'' She stalked away.

Heaven almost giggled out loud when Tab clicked his heels, military style, and took command. He signaled to two volunteers who were frozen nearest to the spot.

"Would you be so kind as to get a bucket of water and some towels and sponge Chef La Sala off? Just try to get the major hunks of meat off him and do something about his hair.''

"I bet Bo has a change of clothes in the wagon. He'd lend you a shirt,'' Heaven suggested.

Tab turned towards her and gave a grim nod. "Good idea, Heaven. I rode up on the bus, so if one of you local residents who drove your own car would mind taking Sergio to town, I'll ride along. Just give me five minutes.'' The volunteers nodded and took charge of Sergio. The man was knocking ribs off Sergio while his wife dabbed at Sergio's hair with a damp cloth. Heaven had to stop watching before she started laughing. No matter how ugly the scene had been, it was also like something out of a Three Stooges movie. She turned just in time to see Tab pick up two glasses of wine from the Shiraz tasting table and head for Tony La Sala. Strange, she thought. Someone ruins a party with an ugly scene and you go drink with him?

The tent resembled a killer beehive humming loudly enough to scare an entire South American village. Every eye was either on Sergio or Tony, with whom Tab Garner was now in serious conversation. Heaven was just about to mosey over toward Tab and Tony when Rowland Alexander tapped loudly on his wine glass and brought the meeting to order.

Rowland was not about to let a very expensive public relations event turn sour. His charm saw him through a round of introductions of all the southern hemisphere wineries represented at the event. Then he moved on to some humorous remarks about each of the Best Chef nominees. He introduced Tony as Tony "Stumblebum" La Sala and the crowd laughed nervously. When he recited some of Sergio's achievements, the crowd gave a standing ovation and Sergio waved, hair gummy with bean sauce, as he left the tent with Tab by his side.

While Rowland was doing his shtick, Bo was having his staff circulate bowls of peach-rhubarb crisp topped with homemade ice cream.

Peach-Rhubarb Crisp
Peaches

Peel and slice enough peaches to fill your favorite oven-proof casserole. Before you start with the peaches, squeeze the juice of a lemon or two in your baking dish and try to coat the peaches with the juice as you slice them. Toss the peaches with a dusting of white sugar and flour, about a tablespoon of each. At the end of this step you should have a baking dish filled almost to the top with peaches that have been coated lightly with lemon juice, sugar, and flour.

Rhubarb Mixture

Slice 4–6 stalks of rhubarb, depending on the size of your casserole. In a medium sauce pan, simmer the rhubarb, ½ cup water and 1–2 cups sugar until the rhubarb is just soft. The variation in the amount of sugar depends on your sweet tooth and the size of the batch. Pour the rhubarb over the peaches and toss together.

Crisp Topping

1 stick butter
1 cup each flour, brown sugar, and oatmeal

½ cup molasses
dash cinnamon

In a heavy sauté pan, melt the butter, add all the
other ingredients and simmer 5 minutes until everything is mixed and hot. You need to do this after your
fruit is sliced and prepared. The trick is to let the topping mixture cool enough to not burn your fingers but
still be pliable enough to spread over the top of the
fruit (about 5 minutes of cooling). The topping is
sticky, but work it over the fruit in a layer, trying to
cover to the sides of the casserole. If a few peaches
stick out of the topping, don't worry. The topping will
spread slightly during baking.

Bake at 350 degrees for about 50 minutes, until the
top is brown and the mixture is bubbling.

Heaven found the Kansas City cadre and plopped down
beside them.

"What a bunch of divas. Is this someone's chair I've
taken?"

Chris squeezed her hand. "No, it was Tab's, but I don't
think we'll be seeing him anymore tonight. We were so
thrilled to see your red head up close to the action. We want
details!"

Heaven gave them what they wanted.

TEN

MURRAY grabbed Mona's hand as they brought her down the final steps of the ladder.

"You're making too much of this, Murray. I could've walked down once they got me loose," Mona said bravely. She was on a stretcher with her leg in a rubber cast. "I know it's not broken."

"Yeah, well, I believe you," Murray said. "But it sure is swollen and bruised. You need to go over to the med center and have them check you out." He looked at the purple and blue cuff of bruises already forming around Mona's ankle. "And putting your weight on it climbing down a ladder could have really torn something."

Mona waved her hands at Murray like she was shooing away a bird. "Are you implying I'm fat? Then, Murray Steinblatz, you're the one who's going to need the paramedics."

Sal patted Mona's shoulder as both he and Murray walked beside her to the ambulance. "There, Murray. That's our Mona. Feisty as usual. Now I know you're OK." Sal had a look that could almost be described as tender, except for the cigar stub hanging out of his mouth.

The scene had reached gothic proportions. The fire department had come in a large hook-and-ladder truck. It had been easy for them to knock another small chunk out of the roof and loosen Mona's foot. But they didn't want to move her until the emergency medical team arrived. The medics, of course, used their own ladder and equipment to bring Mona down. At the same time, the refrigeration man had gone back up on the restaurant roof to replace the bent part. At some point someone must have called the owner of the building and now he was there, happy that his building wasn't burned down, but yelling at everyone about how Mona shouldn't have been up on the roof in the first place. There were more ladders and emergency personnel and yelling than at a genuine three-alarm fire.

By this time the temperature on the ground was well over ninety and it was more like one hundred up on the roof. Everyone, especially the firemen in their rubber gear, was flushed and red-faced.

Murray thought he was going to faint. Somehow this was all his fault. There were onlookers aplenty. The waiters Pauline hadn't been able to get in touch with had come in for their lunch shifts and had stayed for the drama. Sal's customers who had read the note on his door came over, as did Mona's cat store customers and some of the restaurant's lunch customers. Robbie had brought out a big Cambro of ice water and pitchers of iced tea. Brian had made sandwiches with Italian salami, ham, and provolone cheese. There was a carnival atmosphere, made more jolly by the fact that Mona didn't seem to be seriously hurt.

"I'll be back in a jiffy, Murray. Put a sign on the door. And tell old man Nelson this would never have happened if he had used a good roofer," Mona said as they closed the door of the ambulance.

Murray turned to Sal, almost in tears, "Heaven is going to kill me."

Suddenly Sara Baxter stuck her head out the back door of the restaurant. She worked the grill at night, but she had promised Heaven that she would come to work early while Heaven was gone. "Well, she won't kill you yet because she called a little while ago and I told her everything was fine.

It won't do any good for her to know about the air conditioning and Mona 'cause she can't do anything about any of
it. And that particular crisis is all over now. The air's back
on and Mona's going to be OK.''

Murray gave Sara a grateful yet pitiful smile. ''Thank God
you answered the phone. I probably would have spilled
everything right away.''

Sara acknowledged her superior stature under fire. ''I
know. Don't you want to know what I meant by '*that* particular crisis' is over?''

Murray felt another sinking spell coming on. ''What's the
next crisis? Is that what you're trying to tell me? There's
another crisis?''

Sara smiled grimly. ''The Auto Club just called. The national dining team will be here to give us a rating, sometime
this weekend. I tried to talk them out of it. I said Heaven
was out of town, and she would want to be here. I tried
everything I could think of, but it didn't work. It's this weekend or not at all. And we won't know when. They just ap-
pear.''

Sal looked at Murray and shook his head. ''I've got to go
back to work. You're right. Heaven's going to kill you.''

ELEVEN

IT was ten o'clock. Chris, Joe, and Heaven were sitting around a campfire with Bo and his crew. Heaven was eating ribs and throwing the bare bones in the fire. "Rib number six. I was starved. I somehow missed eating in all the furor."

"Well," Bo Morales said, passing a bottle of tequila over to her, "you sure earned your keep, my friend. And Chris, Joe, thanks for staying and helping us pack up. We'll all ride back in the pickups. My cousin is going to camp up here tonight. We don't want to drive the horse trailer and the flatbed down that road at night. It was scary enough in the daytime."

Joe threw a little leftover coffee in the direction of the flames. "I wasn't ready to leave anyway. Even though it's cold, I wanted to be here. This place really has power. And I sure wasn't ready to get in one of those minibuses and listen to the dirt on the party all the way to Aspen. That would have been the longest twenty minutes of my life."

Heaven took a swig of tequila and passed the bottle. "I guess it didn't qualify as a food fight 'cause only one person threw food. Whatever it was, it was very ugly. Those two are bad news. Bo, honey, be careful around them."

Bo held up the tequila bottle in salute. "Don't worry about me. Let's not even talk about it. You stayed up here on the mountain to avoid that trash. Look around instead.''

The moon was almost full, and reflections off the snow higher up the mountain created a glorious shimmering light. Bo had also lit glass kerosene lamps and between them and the moonlight and the campfire all vestiges of modern life were momentarily forgotten. For a few minutes everyone was quiet in comfortable silence.

Heaven, of course, finally couldn't stand it. Her mind was so full of questions. "Think of those first miners coming across that pass from Leadville. Can you imagine? What compelled them? What would it be like to cross a mountain with no roads, where no one had ever traveled before? And I bet they didn't make it in one day. What do you suppose it was like clinging to the side of this mountain in the dark?" No one had an answer.

One of Bo's teammates started singing a Tejano song that everyone else from Texas seemed to know. Soon they all joined in. This beautiful Spanish tune wafted through the mountain air, echoing on and on. Everyone stared out in the dark, thoughts following the melody up the valley, everyone lost in their own imagining and the song. Heaven felt like the luckiest person on earth. The shining eyes of the others gathered around the fire told her she was not alone. Even Chris and Joe were humming along.

Bo stopped singing for a minute and smiled at Heaven. "Whatever happens Saturday, I have just won the prize."

Heaven put her arms out to Chris and Joe on either side. "So have we."

TWELVE

HEAVEN checked her watch again. "Gentlemen, can you believe it? We're early."

Instead of sitting down for a big breakfast, she and the guys had gone to Paradise Bakery, grabbed a muffin and a latte and eaten on a bench outside the bakery. They were there now, enjoying the cool morning temperature and the sunshine.

"Joe, where are you going first this morning?" Heaven asked.

"I think I'll hit the 'Spanish Wine' class. I don't know much about Spanish wines and drinking at nine in the morning sounds positively decadent."

"What about you, Chris?" Heaven asked. He closed his program as if he had finally made a decision. " 'Gumbo' with Ernest Laveau, then 'Best Wine Values' at ten-thirty." Chris answered.

"You already make good gumbo, Chris," Heaven said. "Remember when we had that Mardi Gras party last year and you made the gumbo?"

"I know, and when I learn from the gumbomeister, mine will be even better. What about you, H?"

"Well, I recall I said I always went to wine classes, but I'm going to hit Sergio's stiff risotto demo."

"Stiff risotto?" the boys said in chorus.

Joe went on. "But risotto is supposed to be soft and creamy and a little runny, isn't it?"

Heaven nodded. "Sergio has done for risotto what some other Italian chef did for polenta. Polenta you can serve runny or you can chill it and slice it and do stuff with it. That's what Sergio does with risotto, cooks it partially, then puts it on sheet pans to chill."

"Then what?" Chris asked.

"That's what I'm going to the demo to find out," Heaven said.

Joe got up and looked down the street. "You'll probably dip it in polyurethane and make jewelry out of it. Come on, Chris, speaking of jewelry made me want to go window shopping."

Chris got up too. "There certainly are enough diamond stores in this town. It looks like Rodeo Drive. Heaven, where shall we meet?"

"Noon at the tasting tent. Have fun, you two," Heaven yelled as they headed off.

Heaven sat and read the *Aspen Times* for a few minutes and then decided to go up early to the cooking demonstration tent where Sergio's class was being held.

Once there, she spotted a small line outside the tent.

I guess everyone had the same idea, she thought. As Heaven drew closer, she could hear the commotion.

"Oh, no. Here we go again," Heaven said out loud. "What's the matter?" she called out to no one in particular.

A permed brunette wearing an expensive but gaudy T-shirt with glitter and lace fumed. "They always open these tents twenty minutes before the presentation begins. It's now ten minutes before nine and the flaps of the tent seem to be locked shut, if such a thing were possible. I have very bad eyesight, and I need to be in the front row. I got up at six o'clock so I could get a good seat. There don't seem to be any volunteers or anything. This is a disgrace."

Heaven took a second look at the whiner, wondering what she could have been doing for three hours to get ready.

Whatever it was, it certainly didn't show. She stepped forward and gave the tent flaps a quick jerk. Something was holding the flaps closed. "I'll just go around to the back," Heaven said in a barely audible voice. She certainly didn't want the whole shrew patrol coming with her.

Heaven slipped away. She remembered seeing trucks backed up to an opening on the south side. When Heaven got there, she ducked down and slipped under the canvas. Even though the sun was bright outside, the interior of the tent with all the flaps down was dim. But Heaven could still tell something was terribly wrong.

The chairs, normally in tidy, neat rows were thrown helter skelter. The walls of the tent were scrawled with graffiti and epithets in English, Italian, and Spanish. The letters were written in something red. The demonstration area was demolished. A mirror, normally placed over the work table so the participants could see the hands of the chef, was smashed and jagged pieces of glass were scattered about. The food processor looked as if someone had taken a sledgehammer to it. A refrigerator had been pushed off the stage and the contents thrown all over. The sheet pans with the chilled risotto were scattered everywhere. On one of the pans the shape of a body had been carved out of rice. A long French kitchen knife was sticking out of a sign advertising Sergio's appearance. The word "die" had been scrawled across Sergio's picture.

Heaven walked over to the sign. Gingerly, she touched her finger to her tongue and then touched her finger to a red letter D and her lips. It was a familiar taste. She repeated the process just to be sure. "Oh, great," she sighed, tapping at the red letters with her forefinger.

Heaven headed for the front of the tent. The noise level outside had risen and because three hundred people were waiting outside, it was no wonder. She heard someone, most likely a volunteer, say they would go around to the back. Suddenly, as she got closer to the entrance of the tent and her eyes adjusted to the dimness, Heaven saw what was weighing down the tent flaps. It was Sergio La Sala. He looked as if he had been rolled like a carpet to the front entrance. Either someone was going to take him with them and got frightened away, or they wanted to make sure he was the first thing everyone saw this morning.

Heaven bent down closer to see. "At least he isn't dead," she said with a sigh of relief. Sergio was breathing visibly and the gash on his head was covered with fresh blood.

Just as Heaven was about to open the tent flaps and call for help, the brunette with the permed hair and glitter T-shirt jerked the canvas out from under Sergio and tripped her way into the tent.

"Let us in," she screeched.

Lucky for Sergio, who had already had a bad enough morning, the screecher flew over him and landed on Heaven. As Heaven tried to untangle herself, Sergio opened his eyes, tried to raise his head and passed out again.

"I don't blame you a bit," Heaven said.

Tab Garner hurried up the hill. He had intercepted the message over the walkie-talkie about trouble at the cook's tent. He wanted to get there before Linda Lunch did. Her hysteria would be lessened if he already had a handle on the situation when she arrived. He hit Durant Street just as the Aspen police cruiser did. If his ears weren't playing tricks on him, an ambulance siren wasn't far behind. What could have happened that would warrant an ambulance? Not just a little nick with a French knife. Tab saw Heaven Lee standing away from the crowd. He waved at her and felt a wave of relief. She seemed to have a head on her shoulders, as his granny used to say. The police officer stopped and said something to Heaven and then went in the tent.

"What happened?" Tab asked breathlessly.

Heaven put her hand on Tab's shoulder and looked over at the figure on the ground. She seemed a little shaky. "I planned to go to Sergio's class this morning. When I got here, there were people waiting, so I went around to the back and ducked in under the flap. The place is trashed and there's swear words in three languages. Sergio was knocked out.''

"What do you mean trashed?"

"Destroyed. Go peek in. I'm sure they'll want to gather some evidence before they let people in again, but you can get the picture from the door."

Tab boldly marched right in the tent and was there at least thirty seconds before someone shooed him out. He came back to Heaven's side. "You're right. It's trashed. What did the patrolman say?"

"I told him I was the one who called for help. He said stick around and let me get this victim taken care of, then I want to hear your story."

Tab's eyes were darting about. "I've got to get volunteers rerouting these people. Then I've got to call the hotels and see who can put together a clean-up team for me. Will you do one more thing to help?"

Heaven looked expectantly, her eyebrows reaching *I Love Lucy* question-mark arches.

"Will you not mention the scene between Tony and his father last night to the police? I'd hate to lose two Best Chefs in one day.''

"Wouldn't that be a tragedy? I can tell you're very concerned about Sergio. You took all of ten seconds to look at him."

Tab didn't have time for niceties. "Sergio has his eyes open and an emergency team working on him, which is what I'll need when Linda finds out about this. Please, Heaven?"

"OK, OK. I'll just answer the questions and not volunteer any more information, but you can't expect the cops not to find out about the family feud. Everyone in the food world knows about it and almost everyone in the food world is here in Aspen," Heaven said doubtfully.

"Just buy me some time. Tony is giving a class at his restaurant this afternoon. If they haul him away right now, I'll be two classes short. Sergio's going to be OK, isn't he?"

"He has a concussion, that's for sure. But you're right, he

was conscious by the time the police got here.''

Heaven and Tab watched as the emergency medics wheeled Sergio away on a gurney. His fans were grabbing his hand and asking when they could reschedule the class.

Linda Lunch appeared, walking as fast as she could in her tight, black skirt. Tab gave Heaven a desperate look and took off to intercept her. Heaven walked toward the ever-growing team of law enforcement. Someone with a badge proclaiming "Investigations Officer" was eyeing her.

"That's her," yelled the permed brunette. "She's the one that was in the tent alone with poor Sergio."

Linda Lunch ducked into the Ritz and headed for the front desk. Just then a maid came into view and Linda grabbed the sleeve of the young woman's uniform. "You, where are the phones? Where can I get a bottle of water? If you bring an Evian, I'll give you ten dollars," Linda snapped, digging in her pocket quickly for cash and pills. Her joints were still aching this morning, the stiffness of last night hadn't vanished. What's more, her skirt was too damn long for walking around in Aspen. Especially when she was in a hurry. Poor Sergie.

The startled attendant gave Linda a weak smile and pointed toward a bank of payphones. They were almost all in use and as Linda watched, the last phone was picked up by a Gallo wine salesman. Linda headed straight for him, but not before she pressed some money in the maid's hand. "Agua, over there, on the double," she said, pointing in the direction of the phones. That Gallo guy would just have to get off the line. She needed to call the hospital.

THIRTEEN

JOE and Chris stood in front of the tasting tent along with a hundred other people who were also waiting for someone. The tent had opened at eleven-thirty, so at least the long line of eager imbibers had already trailed inside. Joe and Chris had seen Tab briefly between seminars and he had given them the headlines. Now they could hardly wait to get the real scoop from Heaven. They spotted her red hair flying around the corner. She didn't look happy.

"We know," Chris began as soon as she was by their side. "At least we know that there's been trouble."

Heaven gave them a weak smile. "And, of course, I had to be in the middle of it. All I wanted was for us to come out here to Aspen and do our little skit and drink some wine and have a good time. Was that too much to ask? I didn't get to go to one single class this morning."

"So tell us," Joe demanded.

"After we get inside and get a full glass of vino in our hands. I can't think," Heaven whined.

After having their badges checked, the trio walked into an entry tent that served as a gift shop and makeshift office for the festival. There were aprons, chef's pants and jackets, T-shirts, and tote bags for sale. Many of the items were emblazoned with *The Real Dish* logo, the 1940's-style silhouette of a gorgeous babe holding a steaming pie. There was also a table loaded with the cookbooks of participating chefs. Twice a day, one of the famous would autograph their latest bestseller for the crowds. Heaven looked over at the office area hoping to spot Tab Garner. She locked eyes with Linda Lunch instead, who started gesturing for Heaven to come over to her. Heaven quickly looked away and kept going.

"Don't look camera right," Heaven warned. "LL is trying to get our attention and I can't even fathom talking to her. I just got done with one interrogation. I don't want to start another one until I have some wine."

They passed into an open courtyard where vendors were giving away samples of sparkling water, espresso, and ice cream. "This is where you come for help when you have too many wine samples inside the big tents," Heaven explained. "In front of us are the American wines, to our left, European, and on the right, South Africa, Chile, Australia, and New Zealand, along with lots of food vendors. Where shall we start?"

"Chris and I did a total of 'Spanish Wine,' 'Best Wine Values,' 'How to Cook a Whole Fish,' and 'Gumbo' this morning. American whites for a start?"

Heaven started toward the middle tent. "American whites it is."

Inside the big top, a couple thousand wine lovers were rushing around, trying to find the special reserve wine hidden under the tables of some of the wineries. Heaven and company grabbed wine glasses off the pyramid of clean glasses and checked the map of the room.

"I volunteer to take notes for us all," Chris said as he found his pen.

Just then, Charlene Welling, the owner of The Classic Cup in Kansas City, cruised by the group. "La Crema is pouring their reserve. You don't have to beg for it or anything," she reported.

"Thanks, Charlene," Heaven said and gave her friend a hug. The group turned toward La Crema.

Before they could touch a glass to their lips, Heaven felt

someone tugging on her jeans jacket. She knew who it was before she turned around. Linda Lunch snapped at her like a terrier. "Heaven, why did you ignore me back there? I need to talk to you. What in the hell happened this morning?"

Heaven took Linda's hand and removed it from her arm. "And a good afternoon to you too, editor ma'am. I went to Sergio's class and no one could get in, but I did and the place was trashed. Sergio was out cold with a big knot on his head. But you know that. You were there."

"Sergio was being wheeled away when I arrived. I saw the damn mess. I can hardly wait to go over to the Cavern Club and kick Tony's ass. It cost me a thousand bucks to have that red sauce cleaned up in a hurry and I'm going to take it out of his hide."

Heaven shifted uncomfortably. "I'm not so sure it was red sauce. Tony could never make a marinara worth a hoot. Let's go try the King Estates Pinot Gris from Washington."

Linda persisted, following Heaven. "Did Sergio say anything? Does he seem like he'll be all right?"

Heaven took a drink of the Pinot Gris. "He didn't say a word to me, but by the time he left, he was telling the little old ladies he would make up his classes tomorrow. You sure are taking this personally, Linda. Are you and Sergio an item?"

Linda quivered with anger. "You've got to be kidding. This is not personal. This is about not letting these two idiots ruin my festival."

A voice with a Southern accent entered in their conversation. "They didn't." Tab Garner joined them, empty glass in hand.

"Tab, try this Shafer Red Shoulder Ranch Chardonnay. It's a monster," Chris yelled from the next table.

"Where the hell have you been and what do you mean, they didn't?" Linda demanded.

Tab saluted the rest of the party and drank. "The police station. The La Sala feud isn't the cause of your troubles, boss. Tony La Sala is in the hospital, along with his daddy. He checked in, early morning, complaining about nausea and stomach pains. Accused Bo Morales of trying to kill him with bad baby goat. Doctor says he does have all the signs of some food-borne illness.''

Heaven wanted more details. "Early morning? How early? Tony could have done the tent and then gone to the hospital.''

Tab looked skeptical. "I hardly think Tony could have lured his dad down to the tent at one or two in the morning, knocked him out and torn the place apart, then gone to the hospital. For one thing, Sergio wouldn't have still been unconscious and bleeding when you found him if he had been there since two. But you have a point. I didn't get the exact time Tony checked into the hospital. Sergio says he didn't see his attacker. Of course, he could be protecting his kid but after the stunt Tony pulled last night, that hardly seems likely. There's evidence pointing in another direction.''

Linda grabbed his shirt. "You little weasel. Tell us!''

Tab grinned with triumph. He had made her beg. "The red substance that all the trash was written with wasn't marinara or blood or paint. It was barbecue sauce.''

But of course Heaven knew that.

FOURTEEN

HEAVEN, Chris, and Joe were walking down Mill Street eating ice cream.

"Wow, what a lunch," Chris said. "White wine, ice cream, and a news bombshell."

"So do we think Bo did it? You knew about the barbecue sauce, didn't you? I saw your sneaky eyes when Linda was calling it marinara," Joe said.

Heaven looked at him like he was an unfaithful lover. She was going to ignore his astute assumption for a minute. "Of course, we don't think Bo did it. Bo has more sense than to take out two of the Best Chefs with barbecue-related products. If Bo was guilty, it would have been graffiti in salsa or Cajun spices. No, someone is obviously setting Bo up. And I won't have it. Just because he comes to this contest through an untraditional route, doesn't mean the food snobs can gang up on him. And yes, I knew because I tasted the stuff, a D in the word 'die,' actually."

Joe patted her shoulder. "I didn't mean to get you in an uproar. I don't want them to be mean to Bo either. But Ernest is a good old boy from Houma and Lola Castro started her cafe with twelve seats. Hardly food snobs."

Logic was not going to deter Heaven right now. She stopped at the corner of Mill and Main, across from the Hotel Jerome. She looped her arms through both young men's arms and squeezed. They saw something coming they probably wouldn't like. "Uh-oh, she's trying to be sweet," Chris said with worry in his voice.

Heaven smiled. "So my reasoning is a little faulty. I'm so glad you brought up those two. I want you, Chris, to go to Lola's seminar this afternoon. I think it's 'Twelve Ways to Cook a Plantain.' See what you think about her. Joe, you go to the gumbo class."

"No," Joe said, stomping his foot. "Chris already went and I hate okra."

Heaven batted her eyes. "Joe, baby, this morning when Chris went we didn't know we had a mystery to investigate. Chris can't tell us if Ernest Laveau is crazy."

Chris jumped in. "I beg to differ, I know Ernest is at least weird. That Cajun dialect is impossible to understand, he laughs at his own jokes and they aren't funny, plus all his kin are helping him and they look like extras from *Deliverance*. I read the article about him in *Newsweek*, the one that called him the next Paul Prudhomme. Paul must have fallen off his electric cart when he read that."

Joe was defeated. "I know, I know, with a description like that I'm doomed to Gumbo 101."

Heaven hugged him. "It does sound promising, doesn't it? Ernest can send his evil second-cousin henchmen out to do his vile deeds. I like it. Chris, we have something else important to discuss."

Chris glanced at his watch. "Gosh, Heaven, gotta go if I'm going to make the plantain fest."

"No, you don't," Heaven said firmly. "First, tell me here in front of God and your best friend that you didn't do something terrible to Tony."

Chris looked guilty, but shook his head no vehemently. "I would have, if I'd had a chance, but I didn't. I wasn't prepared to poison Tony last night for his offense two years ago. I can't say I'm sorry he landed in the hospital with a tummy ache though."

Joe turned to Heaven. "He wouldn't tell us if he had.

Chris is a much better liar than you and I. Now, if you want us to go to our assignments you better stop this interrogation."

Heaven tried staring Chris into a confession. He remained silent and had by now adopted an innocent look. He was a performance artist, after all. She gave up. "OK, that's all for now, comrades. Don't forget Rowland has asked us out to dinner tonight and we have practice at five."

Chris wasn't going to let her get away so fast. "Wait a minute, young lady, two things. You don't really want us to come with you to dinner, do you?"

"Yes. This is something Rowland wants to do to thank you for your participation. He knows a free trip isn't really free and you're missing tips. What's the matter? Do you have a date?"

"Well," Chris mumbled, "Tab did say something about doing something. It's the only night there isn't an official event."

"How about this compromise," Heaven offered. "Tab comes to dinner with us and you two can leave the party as soon as dinner is over. No small talk over coffee required."

Chris could live with that. "Good compromise. Second point of business. What trouble are you off to get into?"

"I'm going to find Bo and warn him. I'm sure he won't know about his being a suspect. He's doing a wood demonstration, the properties of apple versus oak for slow cooking, that kind of thing. It's down at Hallam Lake."

"Where's Hallam Lake?" Joe asked. "It sounds like you're getting a better assignment."

"I'm the boss. Once in a while I deserve the cushy stuff, if you can call telling a friend he's a suspect in an assault cushy," Heaven explained. "The so-called lake is a natural environment right in the middle of town. It's just down Mill Street and then left on Puppy Smith. I haven't been down there in years. Sol Steinberg and I met Elizabeth Paepcke at Hallam Lake the year before Sol died."

"And she is?" Chris asked.

"Elizabeth and her husband Walter rediscovered Aspen when it was almost a ghost town in the late forties. They brought their University of Chicago friends out here, purchased abandoned houses. They created what they called The Aspen Idea, in capital letters."

"And that would be?" Joe piped.

"To create a place where mind, body, and spirit could all get a workout, ski a slope, write a novel, sing an opera, that kind of thing. That was the goal of the Paepckes and their intellectual friends. Even if no one hears about the cultural side of Aspen now that the celebrity side is so popular, the Design Conference, the Music Festival, and the Aspen Institute are still going strong. They're part of the original Aspen Idea."

Chris looked at his watch again. "The Aspen Idea. Cool. We now have two minutes to get to our demos. See you later." The three scattered in three different directions.

Heaven quickly walked down the street and slipped through the entryway to the nature center. She wound her way along a trail on the lake side, down to a bench by the water.

Suddenly a hand came around from behind her back with a stick in it, an offering that made Heaven's blood chill. She got up and turned around. "What are you going to do, Bo, knock off a few rich folk with oleander hotdog sticks?"

Bo bowed his courtly little bow and held her hand graciously as she came around to his side of the bench. He led her toward the area where he was giving his workshop. "Since our little run-in with oleander last year, I've included it in my wood class as a warning to campers who think any wood is fine to make a fire."

"Yes, we almost learned the hard way, didn't we, Bo? When those oleander logs ended up in the woodpile in the final round of the Barbecue World Series we almost . . ."

Bo interrupted with a laugh. "Everyone was dropping like flies from the poisonous fumes. Barbecue Village looked like a war zone. Thank goodness you got there in time to warn us. It could have been a lot worse."

''And remember later that night when everyone was in the hospital and we had a party in Aza's room? What a weekend. I'll never forget it, that's for sure.''

Bo looked at Heaven with a question in his expression. ''You were deep into yourself when I stuck that oleander stick in your face. A penny for your thoughts.''

Heaven smiled and let her body lean against him as they walked. It felt good. ''One of my husbands was a friend of the woman who gave this natural area to Aspen. The last time I was at this lake, they were both with me. Now they're both dead.''

Bo still didn't know they had more immediate problems than personal history. ''My poor darling,'' he said. ''You have had a lot of pain. Let me . . .''

Heaven shook her head. ''Can it, Bo. We have no time for regrets or nostalgia. Someone is trying to frame you for all the things that have gone wrong since the festival started. Tony La Sala went to the hospital and says you gave him food poisoning with the cabrito. Then his father is attacked, knocked unconscious, and the tent was decorated with graffiti written with barbecue sauce in Spanish.''

Bo sat down hard on a bench. ''Have you heard of anyone else getting sick?''

''No, I haven't. I even ate some cabrito myself, before the dozen or so ribs, and I'm fine.''

''But he accused me? I don't even know the guy. I'd never laid eyes on him until yesterday.''

''Tony is bad news, just like I told you last night. The Sergio thing is a little more serious. He was hurt.''

''I wouldn't hurt Sergio. I respect him. Heaven, I've seen Hispanics all over Aspen. I'm not the only one in this town who knows Spanish. Anyone could have bought some barbecue sauce and . . .''

''But it wasn't just some store-bought sauce, Bo. It was your sauce. I tasted it and recognized it. Linda had the tent washed down immediately so it could be used this afternoon, but somehow the police know that it's barbecue sauce, not spray paint. If they were smart, they could ask you for a sample of your sauce.''

Bo got up and continued getting ready for his class. He had all the good slow-cooking woods displayed and identified, as well as the dreaded oleander. He had three different kinds of cooking rigs lined up so he could show how to build a fire, as well as what to build it with. ''There were over a hundred people at the party last night. It wouldn't be hard for someone to stick a gallon or two of my sauce in their trunk. So you think that because Tony accused me of poisoning him that the police will think I'm out to get the La Salas?''

''The barbecue sauce angle, the Spanish, Tony's severe nausea and vomiting. Someone is setting you up,'' Heaven said firmly. She thought Bo was taking this way too calmly, or was he avoiding the issue of guilt or innocence? ''We have to be prepared.''

Voices sounding down the path told of people coming their way. Bo looked up. ''I hear Mercedes. She smoked up a couple of things out at T-Lazy-Seven, some sausage, ribs, and quail. There's not enough time to have the class actually slow-cook something but I want the folks to taste what they can do at home, or at least what they should aspire to.''

Heaven spotted Bo's sister-in-law, her hands full of boxes of barbecue. Behind her was another visitor, one that Heaven was less happy to see. It was the police officer she had talked to this morning at the tent. The officer was helping Mercedes with her load, carrying a box that smelled like the sausage.

Bo went over and took the box out of his hands, and introduced himself. ''Can I be of assistance?'' he asked with a big smile.

The officer looked at the two of them and nodded. ''I'm Officer Kent Rainey, Mr. Morales. I'm glad that Ms. Lee is here as well. I would really appreciate you two coming down and giving us some prints, for the purposes of elimination of prints at the crime scene. The station is just around the corner and down a couple of blocks.''

Bo cocked his head. "My fingerprints? You know Ms. Lee was at the crime scene. I can understand you asking for her prints, I guess. But what's the purpose of taking the prints of someone who wasn't there? That is a much different request, as I see it."

The investigations officer was cool. He was used to asking tipsy movie stars for their driver's licenses. "You are correct. They are two different requests. We know Ms. Lee touched things in the tent. Having her prints to match up to the ones she left there this morning will eliminate those from further discussion. Your fingerprints will help disprove allegations that you were there. As far as I'm concerned, if no prints of yours match the prints we took from the tent, I'll consider you off the suspect list. And I don't expect to find your prints, Mr. Morales."

"Thank you for that vote of confidence, officer. Will you tell me who made the allegations?"

"I can't do that right now, sir."

Bo turned to look at his sister-in-law and Heaven. "I feel I have no choice. I'll help you, or I guess I'll be helping myself, but I have a class in fifteen minutes. Can I make it a little after four?"

"Great. Thanks a lot. And you, Ms. Lee?"

"I'll go now," she said as she got up. Bo enfolded her in his arms and whispered in her ear, "Whoever is doing this, we'll smoke 'em out."

As Heaven walked away she heard the officer make another request that worried her. "Do you think I could try one of these ribs?" she heard him say. She wondered if he'd tasted the red graffiti at the tent like she had, and whether he'd be able to recognize the sauce. Was he hungry or just doing his job?

Linda Lunch hated hospitals. She had feared doctors and their poking and prodding and questions and tests since she was a little girl, although she didn't really know why. Linda hoped Tab, or anyone else who worked for her, never found out that the sight of blood made her dizzy. This morning when Sergio had been wheeled past her with that red gash on his forehead, Linda's stomach had churned. She was lucky she rarely had to go near doctors or hospitals or have blood drawn. As Tab often said, she was too mean to be sick. Of course Tab didn't know that Linda's luck could have recently run out. Here she was roaming around a disgusting hospital when she should be running the world's favorite food festival.

"Well, there you are," Linda muttered to Sergio La Sala as she stood at the open door of his room. "How long are you going to lie there like a lazy bum? I didn't fly you up here just so you could nap all day."

"Hello to you, too." Sergio wanted to come back with an equally cutting remark, but he just couldn't. The doctors didn't want to give him any painkillers until they made sure his concussion wasn't serious. Sergio had the worst headache of his life.

"Did that little shit Tony do this to you?"

"No, no. Tony was in the hospital."

"So what? He could've hired someone. The stomach pains could be a cover," Linda pointed out as she perched on the lone chair in Sergio's room.

"How many times do I have to tell the same story? I went down to the tent early to check and make sure I had everything. I wanted plenty of time to go to the store in case I'd forgot something, whatever."

Linda softened a little. She patted Sergio's hand. "Always so organized."

Sergio looked distrustfully at Linda. "I hadn't been in the tent a minute when I was hit from behind. I didn't see anyone or anything, for that matter."

Linda shook her head. "You'd say that even if he spit in your face before he whacked you. Why do you defend the little shit?"

Sergio grabbed Linda's wrist and held it tightly. "Don't

start, Linda. That little shit is my son. That will never change. How is he?''

Linda got up. "He was supposed to be my first stop on this hospital tour, but he's been released. They let him out about one this afternoon so he could do his demo.''

"Good.''

"Don't worry. I'll catch up to him. You, however, have to stay overnight. Sweet dreams, Sergie.''

"Linda, don't do anything until I get out of here. I mean it.''

Linda Lunch walked out of Sergio's hospital room and stopped just out of sight. She couldn't have stayed in there another minute. Her terror was washing over her. Sweat popped out on her forehead. A nurse looked at her with concern. "Can I help you? Do you need some water?'' the nurse asked.

Linda pulled herself together and looked around for an exit sign. "No, there's nothing you can do,'' she said to the nurse as she headed for the door.

FIFTEEN

HEAVEN was spent. It wasn't the act of having her finger-prints pulled that had taken her emotions into territory she didn't often go. It was the fact that those fingerprints were on record already. She had been compelled to tell Officer Kent Rainey, who she now knew was a very polite gentle-man, that he would find a match for all her prints with her old ones in the FBI computer. Officer Rainey didn't seem the least bit shocked by finding out another criminal was roaming the streets of Aspen.

Even the short version—I was a lawyer for rock-and-roll bands and arranged a cocaine deal and my supplier was wired by the feds and I can't be a lawyer anymore but I didn't go to jail either—left her drowning in regret. Telling herself it was different back then didn't help.

Aimlessly, she walked into the Hotel Jerome and plopped down in an overstuffed lobby chair. In ten seconds flat, tears were running down her face. She wasn't sobbing, she just couldn't stop the tears from escaping. She sat there like a leaky faucet, trying to be quiet. Once in a while a little sob would pop out, but the food and wine revelers didn't seem to notice her tears. After a few minutes, a pretty woman from the concierge desk walked over and put her hand gently on Heaven's shoulder. "Can I help you?" A weeping woman in the lobby of the hotel may have not bothered the festival goers, but it had attracted the attention of the hotel management.

Heaven wiped her eyes. ''I just found out that my little dog died back home in Kansas City. Could I please have a phone?''

Motherly clucking commensurate with the gravity of the situation accompanied the delivery of the phone. Heaven never even considered telling the truth. She had spilled her guts at the police station. That was enough for one day.

Heaven hesitated. She wanted to call Hank, but it seemed too corny. Huy Wing, Hank to his Caucasian friends, had been in Heaven's life for almost two years now, but Heaven tried to think of their relationship as very temporary. If she had a flat tire, or a crisis at the cafe, or a day when she felt blue, she might think of asking Hank for help, but rarely would she actually do the asking. Calling him from out of town, especially when things weren't going well, seemed an imposition on Hank's life. In her heart she knew Hank would love to be asked to help, whatever the problem. But then it would be more like a partnership than Heaven could handle.

The fact that Heaven was some twenty years older than he was had never seemed to bother Hank a bit. After all, Hank had pursued Heaven, not the other way around. But she feared that he was teased about her age when he was with his Viet friends and knew for a fact his mother disapproved of their relationship. Sometimes she pictured him at the hospital with all the other young doctors who were getting married, having their first babies. Did it make him secretly embarrassed? Why was it that when the roles were reversed, an older man saw himself as an asset to a younger love, but Heaven felt like such a detriment?

Hank and his mother and sister had fled Vietnam, his father had been killed, he had seen an end to life as he knew it when he was four years old. It prepared him to live for the moment better than Heaven could. Hank's future was always on her mind. She wanted him to have a wife who could have children with him, buy one of those big houses in the burbs, take the family to Disneyland. She also hated that idea, the idea of him happily married to someone else, out of her life. There was one more year of residency left. Then she would have to let go. But until then, Heaven picked up the phone and dialed. Her face lit up when he answered.

"Hi, doctor. I miss you."

Murray Steinblatz was pacing. He had fussed over every knife and fork on every table, lining them up with military precision. He had polished glasses, cleaned the bathrooms himself, even though that was part of Robbie's chores, sprayed the mirrors behind the bar with blue stuff twice. But Murray couldn't provide the one thing that was at the heart of the cafe's popularity. He couldn't provide Heaven. The rating team might not know Heaven, and how her spirit was so important to everyone who worked there, but the staff would know. The drinks tasted better, the food was more delicious, the diners had a better time when Heaven was around.

Sara Baxter came out of the back of the house and watched Murray pacing for a minute. "Murray, go home for a couple of hours. You've been here since early this morning and you have to close tonight. Go lay down."

Murray was busy aiming a fan away from the windows. "I've got four of these going," he muttered. "I think by tonight it'll be OK in here. It won't be chilly, but it'll be OK."

Sara walked up to her friend and put her hands on his shoulders. "It was fine in here at lunch. We'll do the best we can. This restaurant rating team is out of our control. The restaurant will survive. We don't even know that they'll show up tonight. By tomorrow it will be down-right cold in here."

Murray's mind was hopping from detail to detail. "What's the fish tonight, Sara?"

"Sea bass with red curry sauce, jasmine rice, and mango. Murray, take a break."

The phone rang and Murray jumped like a skittish colt. "I think I can take ten more reservations," he said as he went for the phone. "Cafe Heaven."

It was Heaven and she didn't sound happy. "Murray, I just talked to Hank and he said there were fire trucks and ambulances and all kinds of shit in front of the restaurant yesterday. He saw them on the way to the hospital."

"Hi, Heaven." Murray looked desperately at Sara who ran her hand across her neck, as in off with your head, and went back in the kitchen.

"Murray, I called and talked to Sara yesterday and she said everything was fine. What's the deal?"

"Sara didn't want to upset you since there wasn't anything you could do anyway."

"Murray, don't make me come back there and hurt you. Tell me what happened."

"Well, the air conditioner went out during the night Wednesday night."

"And this required a fire truck to fix?"

"And it was just a bird and it only cost four hundred dollars to get running again."

"And the bird required an ambulance?" Heaven was getting worried.

"Mona is the daughter of a heating and cooling company family and she went up on the roof to make sure they did things right."

"Oh, my God. Murray, is Mona all right? She didn't fall, did she?"

Murray was thrilled that Heaven had jumped to a conclusion that was worse than the truth. "No, she didn't fall exactly. She went over to her roof to pick up some trash and her leg got caught in a hole and the rescue team from the fire department had to get her off the roof. But her leg isn't broken."

"Murray, Mona is older than you or me. How could you let her get up on a roof?"

"She was being macho. She wanted to be up there, honest.

She didn't want the air conditioning man to take advantage of us and I was worried and you were gone."

"If her leg isn't broken, what is it?"

"Just sprained and bruised. She was back at the store by three yesterday. And she fell in the hole over on her roof, not ours." Murray knew that sounded cold-hearted, but it was an important point.

Heaven wasn't buying it. "But she was up there in the first place to help us. I'll call her later. Is there anything else?"

Murray felt sweat popping out on his forehead. He gulped. "We were closed for lunch yesterday. It was so hot inside we thought no one would stay, so we saved on the food prep or at least on food. But last night was busy, a hundred thirty or so."

Heaven's voice softened some. "Good thinking about closing for lunch. I'm sorry you had to be in charge when things went wrong, Murray. It's no fun, I know. What about tonight?"

Murray felt his throat closing up. "What about tonight?"

"Do you have lots of reservations?" Heaven asked impatiently. Sometimes Murray could be so dense.

"Yeah, about a hundred fifty. It should be a good night. But we sure miss you. Are you having fun?"

"Depends on your definition of fun. I'm sitting in a hotel lobby, crying. It's time for me to pick up the guys. I guess the Cafe Heaven crisis line is over. I better get off the phone."

"Crying? What are you crying about?"

"Oh, nothing, Murray. Just the past. I'll talk to you tomorrow."

"Wait, Heaven. What's going on?"

"It would take too long, Murray. Talk to you tomorrow." Heaven hung up and went to meet Chris and Joe. It perked her up to know they were missing her at home. Hank too said he missed her terribly. I'm glad they've had some problems, especially since no one got seriously hurt and the air conditioner got fixed for under a thousand bucks. Maybe now the whole crew will understand what I go through, she thought.

Murray stared at the phone for a long time. He'd done it again, kept something from her. But if Heaven knew the Auto Club examiners were on their way, she'd have more to worry about. It didn't sound like Aspen was the dream vacation she wanted, or deserved for that matter. He would just have to handle things here.

Murray took a damp rag over to the front door. When he had been talking to Heaven he'd spotted a couple of fingerprints smudging the paint. Now where did they go?

SIXTEEN

"WE accomplished nothing."

"That's not true. We had a great rehearsal. You make a terrific male waiter, Heaven."

Heaven grinned. "My personal favorite role is when I get to play the temperamental chef."

Joe nodded. "Yeah. I just bet it was. Don't get any ideas for real life."

Chris bounded down the stairs. "How do I look?"

Heaven and Joe circled Chris like photo assistants on a fashion shoot. "Black silk shirt. Black pleated pants. Oriental silk vest. Very nice," Heaven proclaimed.

"My vest," Joe claimed.

"It's nice to know that between the three of us, we can put together one good outfit," Heaven quipped. "Let's go."

As they headed for the door, there was an urgent, insistent, loud knocking. Heaven opened it and the three of them were suddenly face to face with Trixie Malone, star of the silver screen. She was crying.

"I'm sorry to bother you. I thought it was Peter," Trixie said with a catch of her breath and a cute little sob on the end of her speech. At that moment Chris and Joe were both trying to figure out how she'd done that combination catch and sob.

Heaven stepped away from the door. "Oh, please, come

in. I'm Heaven Lee. This is Chris Snyder and Joe Long. We're from Kansas City and Mr. Cooper has lent us his home for the food festival. What are you here for? I mean, what can we do to help you? You look upset."

Trixie didn't seem to notice that Heaven had just been semirude. "It's Picnic," she howled, new tears falling down her beautiful cheeks.

Joe responded this time. "The remake you won an Academy Award for?"

"No, my Pekinese. I named her after the movie. Picnic has been so naughty lately. This is the second time this week she's run away. The first time the staff was able to find her, but they've gone home. I'm not entertaining, of course, because no one's in town. It's June. I let everyone leave early and now I don't know how to find my little darling." On cue, Trixie let out a precious sob. The three spectators sighed. She was so cute.

Heaven glanced at her watch. It was definitely a case of a damsel in distress. The two young men were already on the case. They had moved quickly out the door and up the road yelling, "Here, Picnic!" for all they were worth. Any dummy could figure out that it would be advantageous to find the movie star's pet. Joe and Chris were no dummies.

"We only have a few minutes before we have to leave, but if Picnic doesn't turn up, we'll alert the guard when we head out and they can send a search party to help you," Heaven said in as kind a tone as she could muster.

Trixie looked at Heaven as though Heaven were Albert Einstein on a good day. "What a great idea. I guess I'm so used to having lots of people around, I just am no good in a crisis anymore."

Heaven wagged her finger at Trixie Malone. "You can never be too famous or too rich to get yourself out of a jam. Let's go look on the side deck, where Peter's lap pool is."

Sure enough, when Trixie and Heaven opened the doors onto the side deck, there was a tiny, ratlike creature paddling around in the lap pool. "Picnic, you scared Trixie, you naughty girl!" The dog scampered for the shallow end of the pool and tried to make a run for it, but Heaven would have none of it. She didn't want to have to spend more time catching this pooch again. Heaven scooped the wet dog up and quickly went inside to find a towel, while holding the drippy thing as far away from her clothes as she could. Trixie was following close behind, reprimanding her pet.

"So just because Trixie doesn't let you swim in your pool, you came down here, didn't you? You are too smart, you bad baby."

Heaven held out the shivering mass of clotted hair to her owner. "Just keep the towel to carry her home in."

"The pool boy said her long hair was clogging up the filter system, but I guess we'll just have to find a new pool boy, won't we, Picnic?"

Heaven guided their guest to the front door. She opened it and yelled for the guys. "Joe, Chris, we found it . . . her . . . Picnic."

As they all congregated on the front drive, Heaven knew she needed to make this chance encounter count. "Since you don't have your whole staff and you don't have guests this weekend, why don't you and, ch, Picnic, come down Sunday evening. The food festival will be over by then and we'll cook something wonderful."

Trixie Malone hugged each of them, a treat made less so by the presence of a wet Pekinese in her arms. "I accept. I'll bring the towel back then. Thanks for the invite. I always think I want to come out here and spend quality time alone. I forget how boring actors are in real life, myself included. I'm always tired of my own company after two days. See you Sunday."

"Heaven, why did you say we accomplished nothing this afternoon?" Joe asked as they headed for town. "Everyone went to their stupid assignments."

"I ended up giving my fingerprints to the police and confessing I was a felon," Heaven said. "Bo did too, not the felon part but the fingerprint part. You both have heartburn from all the gumbo and fried fruit you consumed and neither of you found a secret stash of paintbrushes and barbecue sauce conveniently hidden in Ernest or Lola's supplies. I'd call that a wash. And don't forget the air conditioning and Mona problem at home."

"Very nice how you got Rowland to take us to the Cavern Club, where Tony La Sala cooks," Chris said with grudging admiration as they pulled into valet parking.

"Except he won't be there tonight so we can snoop better," Joe predicted.

Heaven pulled a five dollar bill out of her handbag. "As much as I'd like to take credit, it wasn't hard to get Rowland to agree to this place. Everyone wants to see and be seen at the Club during the festival." She relinquished the car and money to the valet and then gave their names to the doorman. They were ushered downstairs.

Even though the Cavern Club was named after the Liverpool nightclub that incubated the Beatles, the Aspen version did not resemble, in anything but name, the grungy joint in England. The Aspen version was like a posh men's club, dark wood, big chairs, private dining rooms.

Tonight it was packed. Heaven spotted Rowland and Tab at the bar. They seemed to be in deep conversation.

Chris was thrilled to see his new friend. "You escaped," he said to Tab when they neared the bar.

Tab turned around and gave Chris a little hug. Rowland jumped up and gave Heaven a big hug and his bar stool. "Greetings. Tab and I have been trading Linda Lunch stories to work up an appetite. And I ordered us a bottle of Veuve Cliquot to start. I remember you favored it, Heaven. By the way, I checked in at the door and Louie says twenty or twenty-five minutes."

Tab had not waited for the champagne to arrive. He was nursing something that looked like a water glass full of vodka and ice. "I paid off the local publicity coordinator, with the promise of a very expensive dinner at Restaurant Daniel the next time she's in New York, to baby-sit Linda tonight. Money well spent.''

Soon the bartender arrived with five Riedel flutes and their wine. He opened the bottle with the proper whoosh instead of a pop and quickly filled their glasses.

Heaven held up her glass first. ''To the best chef in Aspen. Let's hope he or she is able to enjoy their moment of fame.'' Everyone groaned and toasted and laughed and traded stories. The next thing they knew, their glasses were empty and their table was ready.

As they studied the menu, Heaven idly speculated, ''I wonder if the food will be up to par tonight, what with the chef, and I'm feeling generous in calling him that, in the hospital.''

Joe had been casing the dining room. ''He's not,'' he said, indicating with a jerk of his head what direction to look.

There was Tony La Sala, in spotless chef whites that showed no indication of his having cooked in them, working the room. He seemed fine, laughing with a long table of Italian winemakers.

''Fast recovery,'' Heaven said dryly. ''Too bad he wasn't the one with the knot on his head instead of his poor dad. Does anyone know anything about Sergio's condition?''

Tab looked up from the menu. ''I went over to the hospital and checked on Sergio late this afternoon. They want to keep him overnight, just in case, but if everything goes all right, he'll be released in the morning.''

Suddenly a harried waiter appeared beside them. He had a frightened look in his eyes. There is nothing worse for a server than a house full of food professionals trying to impress each other. The good part was they tipped well. The bad part was everything else. They quickly decided and gave their order.

''I even know what wines we should have,'' Heaven said. ''Rowland, is it OK if we have Burgundies tonight? They have a good list of Burgundies in both red and white.''

"Of course," Rowland replied. "I don't want to taste another one of my own wines until tomorrow morning. We can't grow Pinot Noir grapes successfully in Australia so I enjoy drinking it when I'm here or in France."

Heaven smiled up to the waiter. "Then we'll have this 1992 Montrachet first and then the 1989 Volnay from Michel Lafarge. Volnay is Lafarge's thing. I got to meet him once in New Orleans."

"Good years, and a great grower," Rowland piped in.

Just then Ernest Laveau entered the bar without his entourage of cousins. He sat down at the bar beside a blonde in a minidress and grinned.

"I'm so glad we got a table where we can still see in the bar," Chris said. "The cast of characters is just too good. Ernest looks ready for action tonight."

When their first courses arrived, they started tasting around the table.

Chris looked up with a strange look on his face. "Heaven, taste the scallop saté that Tab ordered."

Heaven slid a caramelized scallop off a skewer.

"Be sure and dip it in that sauce, that's the important part," Chris ordered.

Heaven did as she was told. "Spicy, peanuts, Thai, good."

"That's your Thai peanut sauce. I've served it a million times."

Tab pushed his plate into the middle of the table so Joe and Rowland could weigh in with their opinions, then he dug into the roasted beet and goat cheese on arugula that Heaven had ordered.

Heaven, for a change, was a model of fairness. "You're right, Chris. It does taste like mine. But every Thai peanut sauce tastes like this. There's not much difference in any of them."

Joe pointed accusingly at the plate. "Everyone might have the same peanut sauce, but no one else has this presentation."

Heaven flash-fried oriental rice noodles so they would expand to many times their original size and get crispy. Then she halved an orange, stuck the skewers with the saté, usually pork or chicken, into the orange that was then buried with the crispy noodles. The monkey dish of sauce was nestled in the noodle nest. It had a Sputnik/*My Favorite Martian* look to it. So did Tony's version here at the Cavern Club. Heaven had to concede on this point.

"I like the foie gras that Rowland ordered best," Tab declared and everyone agreed.

"The foie gras was very good with the chestnuts. I wonder whose dish that is?" Chris asked cattily. Heaven gave him a look that said behave. Chris couldn't believe she was defending Tony, the little creep.

"We're easy to please. Just give us fine French wines and foie gras," Heaven joked.

Soon a small army of servers descended on their table and swept away their starter plates to make room for the entrees. They presented the main courses with a flourish. After the oohing and aahing was over there was a brief silence while everything was sampled. Wine glasses were switched and the red Burgundy was poured and declared delicious.

Again Chris looked up from his plate, this time triumphantly. "You may be able to say that all peanut sauce is alike, but you can't say this lamb shank isn't yours. Taste."

This time the whole table stopped eating and dove for Chris's plate. Heaven stabbed a forkful of meat and dipped it in the sauce. This time there was no denying it.

Guinness Lamb Shanks

    4–6 lamb shanks
    a six-pack of Guinness Stout
    a large can of apricot nectar
    2 whole garlic heads
    rosemary, kosher salt, pepper, flour
    oil

Lightly dredge the shanks in flour and brown them in a heavy sauté pan in which ¼ cup of olive or canola oil has been heated. Transfer the shanks to a baking dish and add equal parts stout and apricot nectar, plus salt and pepper. Halve the heads of garlic and add to the pan, cut side down. Throw in some rosemary and bake covered for about two hours at 375 degrees. Uncover, remove the garlic and baste the meat with the liquid. Finish the roasting process uncovered. To brown the shanks and get them fork-tender will probably take another hour, depending on their size. If they are small shanks, uncover after one hour.

These shanks and their cooking sauce are great over mashed potatoes, risotto, or basmati rice. Just squish out some of the garlic on a good loaf of French bread and get ready to sop up the good sauce stuff.

"Sure is tasty," Tab offered. "What's that flavor?"

Heaven reached for one more bite. "I had a cook early on at the cafe who came up with this, braising lamb shanks in apricot nectar and Guinness Stout, along with the usual rosemary and garlic. So little Tony wasn't as stupid as I thought he was. While I thought he was merely a space cadet, he was stealing my best dishes. Who's the dumb one now?" she asked as she got up and headed for the bar.

They spotted Tony schmoozing Patricia Wells and the famous California winemaker Helen Turley at the end of the bar. As the two famous diners walked away, Tony turned to see Heaven bearing down on him fast.

From their table, the four men in Heaven's party had a great view of the bar. Tab rubbed his hands together. "Oh boy. I've never seen Heaven in action, but I have a feeling this will be fun."

Tony La Sala wasn't that pleased to see Heaven. "Well, well, Heaven, I thought I spotted you and Chris last night at the fish fry. What are you doing in town?"

Heaven slammed Tony up against the bar with both hands.

It was a surprise move that almost upended him. "Tonight I'm eating some bad imitations of my own dishes, you little asshole."

Tony straightened up and came out swinging vocally. "Don't kid yourself, Heaven. I don't need your piddly-ass recipes. I'm the premiere chef in the most exclusive club in the most exclusive town in the Rockies, maybe in the country. I'm a star."

A voice boomed from across the room. "So am I, and you'll be seeing stars when I get through with you." It was Nathan Clark, former linebacker for the Miami Dolphins. When Nathan's knees collapsed after a particularly rough football season, he had gone from the backfield to culinary school. Nathan, with hands the size of catcher's mitts, found his true love was creating delicate and beautiful confections out of sugar and chocolate. Now the pastry chef at the exclusive Potomac Club in Washington, D.C., he was at the festival teaching a class in spun sugar. Tony had worked for Nathan too.

Nathan wasn't as kind as Heaven had been. He picked Tony up with one hand by the nape of his chef coat. "This is my caramel turtle, you little pissant, and you better never make another one." With that he took the plate that he held in his other hand and pushed the offending dessert into Tony La Sala's face. An edible animal created out of burnt sugar cake, espresso ice cream, caramel sauce, and spun sugar landed somewhere around Tony's left nostril and was quickly ground into his left cheek by the powerful punch of Nathan Clark.

Heaven caught the ice cream as it moved down Tony's front and gave it a push into his pristine jacket. Then she headed back to the table through an almost silent dining room, leaving Tony to be rescued by his staff who seemed reluctant to take on Nathan Clark. Ernest Laveau was chuckling into his glass, one arm around the waist of the mini-skirted blonde.

When Heaven returned to the table, all four of her dinner

partners were standing to greet her. They clapped and the tension in the dining room evaporated. Noisy laughter and the clanging of glassware resumed. Other tables saluted her with their wine glasses. The waiters started running again.

"Heaven, that's one of the many things I love about you," Rowland said with affection. "There's never a dull moment. Now I think we better order a couple of those caramel turtles. Unless you're a member of the Potomac Club, it's now or never."

SEVENTEEN

AT first, the night had gone great for Murray. His antennae had been sensitive all evening, his timing perfection. When a table emptied he had the next party ready to sit, but he also had kept the bar full all night. The bartenders loved it when they got to sell the first round of drinks to a dining party at the bar. Murray didn't mind transferring the bar tab to the tables, but he always asked the parties to tip the bartender before they left for the dining room. It wasn't that waiters didn't have good intentions to shell over the fifteen percent of the bar tab to the bartenders. It just didn't always get done at the end of a long, busy night.

Murray had spotted the Auto Club food tasters as soon as they came in. Not that he had said anything to them, of course. And they certainly didn't introduce themselves to him. The woman from the club office who had called yesterday said the team usually let their presence be known after they ate, then later phoned back to the restaurant to ask specific questions about certain dishes. Murray just had a feeling about this couple. They looked official. He spotted them writing on small notebooks several times during the night and they had asked lots of questions, especially about the wine list. They had also ordered well which was a big relief to the kitchen. You can't show your stuff if the customer wants a well-done steak or a plain piece of fish. The woman had asked for a chicken dish to be altered slightly and Murray was actually glad at that moment Heaven wasn't around. Sometimes Heaven was pissy about doing that kind of stuff. Murray figured it was part of the Auto Club test to see if you were willing to accommodate special diets.

The staff had been on their best behavior all night. He had explained the importance of getting a good Auto Club rating and had also explained they wouldn't know ahead of time which night the inspectors would be dining. He told them everything he knew, about how they rated the bathrooms, the glassware, the dishes, as well as food and service. When the prime suspects came in, Murray whispered in everyone's ear, made sure to give them the best of everything. He also alerted the kitchen, which he knew was chancy. Sara huffed and said, "Like we don't give our best to every guest?" But Murray noticed the plates that went to that table looked extra nice and the portions seemed large.

It was almost ten o'clock. Carmen McRae was singing with Dave Brubeck on the sound system. Only a few tables were empty. The cafe had the feel of a village place tonight, as in Greenwich Village. Murray and Eva had lived near Sheridan Square and even though he had no stomach for New York any more, he sure did miss that neighborhood. Just as his mind wandered back to his past, a part of his present walked in the door. The perfect evening at Cafe Heaven was now in jeopardy.

Jumpin' Jack, usually somber and stoic in his camo garb, was highly agitated tonight. He was hugging the sides of the wall and working his way around the dining room perimeter. Of course, many tables were around the dining room perimeter so this meant encounters with the dining public. Jack was in his SWAT team stance, arms in a defensive posture in front of him.

The Auto Club inspectors stood up and looked alarmed.

Other diners thought Jack was some performance artist who had mistakenly come for the open mike night on Friday instead of Monday. Murray was trying to get his hands on

Jack without alarming the whole room. Jack kept moving and Murray sauntered as fast as he could in his direction. If only people wouldn't stop him to talk about their food or ask where Heaven was tonight, he could get close enough to grab Jack by the arm and take him out the back door. Finally, when Murray saw Jack heading straight for the Auto Club rating team, he stopped trying to be subtle and started trotting across the dining room floor.

Jack had on black face makeup and some sort of Ninja getup. He could have been mistaken for a truly dangerous person instead of just the mildly delusional one he actually was. Suddenly Jack pointed up to the ceiling. "Hear them? Hear them? They're on the roof! Everybody take cover. It's Saddam Hussein," he shouted as he grabbed the female member of the inspection team and shoved her under the table.

EIGHTEEN

"WHERE do I go from here?" Joe asked. He and Heaven were alone in the van. The two had left Chris and Tab at the club, then dropped Rowland reluctantly at the condo he shared with the other Aussies. Rowland thought it a much better idea to go up on the mountain with Heaven for the night.

"Turn left on the other side of the bridge. There's the parking lot," Heaven instructed. They were already halfway home when Heaven begged for a detour. She really needed the sound of rushing water to clear her head. They had retraced their steps and headed out of town for a little park on Cemetery Road, just on the outskirts of Aspen. "This is the Harry Stein Park. It meets up . . ."

Joe stopped the explanation. "I can't believe you wanted to come to a place named Harry Stein, on purpose." Harry Stein was the name of a Kansas City police detective who loved to give Heaven a hard time.

"I know, but I had a couple of lovely hours here two years ago, before I found out the name. This Harry Stein must have been a much nicer person to have such a perfect place named after him. The Roaring Fork River is right down here and there's a bench somewhere, yeah, right there," Heaven said as she and Joe groped their way to the river's edge. The white noise of water enfolded them. Joe put his arm around

Heaven like they were on a date. She sighed and tried to release the worry of the day with her breath.

"There's nothing like a relaxing dinner with friends, a quiet, calm dinner," Heaven said with enough sarcasm to ice over the stream.

Joe looked at her. "I wonder how many more restaurants Tony borrowed from? What an idiot. He could have made caramel bunny rabbits or changed the lamb shanks to veal shanks."

"The dish doesn't work with veal. The ale is too heavy," Heaven said distractedly.

"I was just making the point that Tony isn't very bright to take the dish as is, and transplant it to his menu."

"Oh, honey. I was far away. I know what you were getting at, of course. Tony is a thief who thought it was safe up here in the mountains. Like none of us would ever venture into his fancy-schmancy world."

"What do you think really happened with Sergio and Tony, H?"

Heaven closed her eyes. "I don't know why I can't shake the feeling that Tony had something to do with his dad's attack. He lives here. He could probably find someone to do the job for money, while he was inducing vomiting at the emergency room."

"I hate to ask, but do you think Bo could have anything to do with this mess?"

"I guess Bo or Lola or Ernest aren't off the short list. We feel close to Bo because of what happened last year at the barbecue contest, but he is ambitious and proud of it. Who knows how that will shake out in the Best Chef contest. I feel pretty cynical right now. This is all totally unimportant in life's big picture. We're not curing canccr or balancing the budget. We're all just trying to give people an hour of pleasure, an excuse to love each other around a table and a bottle of wine. Why would anyone hurt someone else to get a food award?"

Joe hugged Heaven tight. "People hurt each other for a

lot less, H. Let's go home. We have to perform in the morning."

Before Joe and Heaven could get up, a crash sounded from the bridge. Headlights swerved. Sparks flew as metal scraped the safety wall. A car was careening toward them. It bounced into the parking lot, barely missing Heaven's van and a Land Rover loaded with kayaks. Then it tried to leap down from the parking lot to the bench where Heaven and Joe were sitting. Joe grabbed Heaven's hand and started to run, pulling her with him. All at once the vehicle got hung up on a stump and clouds of smoke billowed out of the wheels. The horn started to blare.

Heaven stopped running. "The driver may be hurt. We better go see."

Joe agreed reluctantly. "Heaven, I know this sounds crazy, but this could be a trick. Maybe this car was trying to run us in the river. Let me be the guy."

Joe and Heaven went up to the car from behind so they wouldn't be hit by rubble or, worse yet, the front end of the car if it didn't hold on its precarious balance. Joe jerked the driver's door open and someone fell out onto the ground. As he reached in to turn off the car, Heaven rolled the inert shape over. It was Ernest Laveau. She knelt down and quickly stood up, her arm fanning the air around her nose.

"Is he . . . ?" Joe's question trailed off in the sound of the rushing water.

"Alive and drunk," Heaven replied. "Jack Daniel's, I think."

Linda couldn't believe she was standing here. Not voluntarily. In a hospital room.

It was dark but she could see Sergio's steady breathing under the covers.

She wasn't sure what had led her to this spot. Certainly not rational thought. After dinner, she had stumbled around town some more, going first to the Ritz, then the bar at the Hotel Jerome. Just as she was getting ready to go up to her room and get some rest, she had instead jumped into her rental car.

Now here she was, sitting in the dark, watching Sergio sleep. He turned toward her, opening his eyes with a start. "What the . . . Linda? Is that you?"

Before she could think about it, Linda slipped silently over to Sergio's bed and got in beside him. "Yeah, Sergie, it's me. Now go back to sleep and don't ask what I'm doing here because I don't know the answer to that. I . . . I didn't want to be alone."

Sergio slipped his arm around Linda's waist and pulled her close. They weren't facing each other so it was easier. "We've got three good hours before the nurse finds you and tosses you out. Lay here and rest."

NINETEEN

"HURRY up. We'll be late." Heaven Lee was stomping around the kitchen with her "script" in hand, really just a list of the points they wanted to cover in their workshop. This acting troupe was counting on improvisation to see them through.

Joe came down the stairs like a diva looking for an encore. Chris goosed him and ran ahead, wardrobe bags and a sack of wigs in his hands.

"Mom, Joe won't tell me the Ernest Laveau story. I want the dirt."

"We were contemplating nature when . . . " Heaven said.

Chris interrupted. "In the dark?"

"It was a Zen thing, I had an urge," Heaven huffed. "Suddenly here comes this car, out of control. It ran into the parking lot and got caught on a stump and we rescued Ernest, who must have spilled a whole bottle of bourbon in the car. Not only did he reek, but the car reeked."

Joe continued. "Heaven went up the street to call the cops and I stayed at the scene. The ambulance and towtruck came and a police patrolman. The last we saw of Ernest he was curled up on the stretcher like it was a kindergarten mat, snoring away peacefully."

"So?" Chris asked.

"So, he lives below sea level on some bayou and probably

didn't know how much the altitude would affect his drinking. Or, the other possibility is the 'Best Chef' menace strikes again," Heaven said as she grabbed her bag. "Whichever it is, we don't have time to mess with it now. We're forty minutes away from curtain time."

Forty minutes later, Tab Garner stood up in front of a full house. The noise in the Hotel Jerome ballroom was only a few decibels below a din as people said hello to friends and took their seats.

Tab did a between-the-teeth whistle that got everyone's attention. "One of the best things about *The Real Dish* festival each year is meeting new talent from around the country. Heaven Lee and her staff at Cafe Heaven have made a name for themselves for having imaginative world food cuisine and for being one of the first cafes in the country to present a venue for talent to perform at an open mike night. They are also well known within the wine community for selling plenty of wine that isn't California Chardonnay or Merlot. Which brings us to Rowland Alexander, Australia's tallest winemaker. Rowland?"

Rowland Alexander stepped forward with his customary presence. "I remember the first time I set foot in Kansas City, Missouri. It was a Monday night, and I had a wine dinner scheduled at Cafe Heaven on Tuesday, so I thought I'd go over and introduce myself. Little did I know I'd find myself in the middle of a packed dining room with performance art and singing and poetry going on. The best part of it for me was the number of wine bottles I saw on tables, and some of those wine bottles were my own.

"The purpose of this training session is to make wine more accessible to our customers. I can't think of better people to help me than Cafe Heaven owner Heaven Lee and the producers of the open mike night, Chris Snyder and Joe Long. I'm sure we'll all see ourselves in these few tips on how not to sell wine." There was applause from the group. Everyone loved Rowland.

Heaven and company had already placed a small table and

two chairs on stage. Heaven and Chris, posing as a middle-aged couple, sat down. Heaven had an unattractive pillbox hat perched on her head and a vintage, ratty fox stole pinned on her shoulders. Chris had on his Rockford-style polyester sports jacket. Joe approached their table with a wine-tasting cup strung around his neck on striped ambassadorial ribbon, wearing a waiter's jacket, pencil over his ear and order pad stuck in the small of his back.

Chris explained that it was the couple's twenty-fifth wedding anniversary and they wanted a bottle of wine to celebrate. Joe then made the couple feel dumb and uncomfortable, asking them varietal and vintage questions they obviously didn't know and using French phrases. Disappointed, Chris settled for a beer and Heaven ordered iced tea. Joe left the table triumphant, his superior knowledge proven once again.

Then the trio briefly replayed the same scene. This time Joe's wine steward was friendly and helpful, getting the couple a bottle of sparkling wine from California for under thirty dollars.

Next, Joe and Chris played an adventuresome couple who wanted to try something new, maybe a Spanish wine, or one from Australia. Heaven was the befuddled server, who only knew about California cabernet.

In the next skit, Joe appears as Josephine, in a short Eva Gabor wig and a female power suit jacket. As the female host of a business dinner party that evening, Joe had taken the time to stop at the restaurant ahead of time to study the wine list and ask for recommendations. The businesswoman was told by Chris, as the janitor, the restaurant didn't open until five and no one could help her.

Next, Heaven played a woman dining alone who was totally ignored by her server, wickedly played by Chris. When she asked for wine by the glass, Chris told her only bottles were available, a lie, and recommended a wine that he would get a bonus for selling.

When Heaven, as hostess, led Joe and Chris to the table,

blowing bubbles with her bubble gum, the audience went wild. Joe and Chris, dressed casually, called after her, asking for a wine list. Heaven stopped to talk to a friend at the imaginary bar, not responding to their plea. Finally, Joe had to get up from his table and approach her, asking for a list again.

Heaven looked him up and down. "You're kidding? You don't look like the type who can afford wine. Gosh, I don't even know where one is. I'll have to go in the office and look." With that she shuffled off, blowing bubbles and leaving Joe high and dry, and wineless.

Heaven soon returned to Chris and Joe's table, attired in a chef's hat and apron. She shook a Chinese cleaver in their faces and told them that they could not have the chardonnay they had ordered with the duck, it would spoil her wonderful dish.

As a grand finale, Joe and Chris appeared in gray, fluffy wigs, with gloves and proper flowered jackets. As they did their *Arsenic and Old Lace* imitation, the room broke out into full laughter. Heaven was decked in a tux jacket and Andy Warhol-style wig, playing the server. The ladies had to beg her for a glass of merlot. "You broads are too old to drink, ain't ya?" Heaven cracked. "This stuff is expensive, ya know. How about some of the house red, instead?"

After this pièce de résistance, the audience was fully relaxed and asked a few questions, one about the availability of the trio to come do their training session at various restaurants.

"You pay. We'll come," Chris quipped and that ended the hour with the appropriate zinger. Everyone was crowding around to add congratulations on a job well done.

Heaven made a beeline for Tab. "Have you heard anything about Ernest this morning?"

"I heard you and Joe had more excitement than Chris and I did."

"Please, I don't want the gory details of your date. Is Ernest going to be able to cook tonight?"

Tab led Heaven slightly away from the crowd. "I went over to the hospital first thing this morning, as soon as Chris called and told me what had happened. Ernest was up and at 'em, with the world's worst hangover. He was going over to the police station to post bond on his DUI charge and then start to work on his food. He was hopping mad though."

"He should be glad to be alive. If it wasn't for us and that stump, we could have found Ernest at the Hoover Dam," Heaven said.

"Ernest has quite a story. Says he went to the Cavern Club and a young, pretty blonde starts talking to him. After the incident with Tony, the blonde says why don't we go to my place where it's more private. Ernest says sure. The blonde, Mindy was the name she used . . ."

Heaven stopped Tab mid-sentence. "What makes you think it isn't her name?"

"Just listen. Mindy tells Ernest she wants to drive her own car home, so she walks him to his car and gets in to draw him a map. She lives out by Woody Creek Tavern, she says. That's when she pulled out a flask of Jack Daniel's and they both had a swig. At least Ernest thinks they both drank. He was pretty distracted by this time, what with the promise of sex in the air. One thing he *is* sure of. When Ernest was handing the flask back, it spilled between the seats. They were laughing and kissing and that's what accounts for the liquor smell in the car. At least that's what Ernest says this morning."

"Does Ernest think, do you think, she slipped him something?"

Tab nodded. "Ernest certainly does. Mindy told him her car was clear over by Waggoner Park so she would meet him at her place. As soon as he started driving, his vision was blurred, he felt woozy. The next thing he remembers was hitting the side of the bridge, which is where you came in. Oh, by the way, he broke his little finger."

"That was probably my fault," Heaven said. "He's a big man and when Joe opened the door and he came falling out,

I wasn't able to break his fall. His hand must have taken the hit. Do you think the map Mindy gave Ernest is still in his car? It would be interesting to see if there really is a Mindy or a house or if she was just sending him on a wild goose chase on a dangerous road.''

Tab glanced at his watch and shrugged. ''I think Ernest is seeing conspiracy theories to cover his ass with his wife back in Louisiana, that's what I think. Are you coming out to the lunch?''

''Of course. Our gig is done. Maybe we can relax and have a little fun.''

''Tell Chris I'll see him out there. I need to run right now and pick up the queen of the ball.''

''Linda?''

''You've got it. She was fit to be tied when I told her about Ernest. Hurry out. The Champagne Council puts on a good party.''

When Tab had left the room, Heaven rushed over to Joe and Chris.

''Guess what?'' Chris bubbled. ''This guy from the National Restaurant Association wants us to do our presentation at their annual convention. It's in Chicago in May. Cool, huh?''

Heaven nodded distractedly. ''Cool. Yeah. Let's go. We're due out at Maroon Bells in half an hour. The French Champagne Council is throwing a lunch for all the presenters and nominees. We've got to plan our strategy.''

''For?'' Joe asked.

''After hearing what Tab learned from Ernest, I'm sure the Best Chef phantom has struck again. That just leaves Bo and Lola. We don't have much time.''

''Come on, Jack. Just a few more steps. I'm right behind you. Let's keep going.'' Murray was talking in his most soothing voice.

He and Jack were climbing the ladder to the roof of Cafe Heaven. It was Saturday morning and Murray had had another sleepless night. The evening before, he had retrieved the Auto Club inspector from under the table, and deposited Jack in the kitchen with instructions to the staff not to allow him back into the dining room.

Murray had then gone back to the front of the house and tried to make the best of a bad situation. Because so few of Cafe Heaven's regular patrons had been alarmed by Jack's little fit, Murray used the performance-art-gone-bad excuse with the inspection team. The professional inspectors were certainly shaken by the event, but they didn't immediately threaten to sue. They did present Murray with a business card that made it clear he had been right about who they were and why they were there. "You'll be hearing more from us," was their parting comment as they made a beeline for the door.

Murray had worried into the wee hours about what Jack had done to their restaurant rating and how to tell Heaven. Now it was morning and he was taking Jack on an inspection tour of the roof to prove Jack's fears were goundless.

Jack swung easily onto the flat roof and Murray cautiously crawled off the ladder, his heart pounding wildly. "See," Murray panted. "Saddam Hussein is not up here, Jack. Neither is Chairman Mao or Attila the Hun."

Jack marched resolutely around the perimeter of the roof, making sure that no one was hiding behind the air conditioner or the generator for the walk-in cooler. Sure enough, he and Murray were the only souls around. Finally he smiled at Murray and sat down next to him.

Murray had not ventured far from where he landed when he crawled off the ladder. He was clutching the raised lip of the roof surface for dear life.

"You know, Jack, everybody has fears. You just can't let them get the best of you. Like I told you last night. You can't take your fears out on the rest of us."

Jack nodded solemnly. "I've made a mess for Heaven. But in my mind, I was so sure the place was being attacked that I thought I was helping. Will they give Heaven a bad grade because of me?''

"Who knows, Jack? We did the best we could. I didn't even tell Heaven the inspectors were coming. Talk about fears, I was scared to tell Heaven a little thing like that. How in the hell do I think I can help you with your fears?''

"She's gonna kill us both,'' Jack said.

Murray slowly got to his feet, sneaking a look at the ground in the process. "If she does, Jack, she'll be putting down two guys who have met their fears. You came up here and saw that no one was up here with a bomb. And I've always been so afraid of heights, but I climbed that damn ladder. Now I'm going to stand up like a man, not crawl around like a baby. I can do this.''

"I'll go with you.'' Jack got up and walked around on the roof with Murray who finally was brave enough to stand near the edge and wave across the street in the direction of Sal's barbershop.

He put his skinny arms up in the air like a warrior. "See, Jack. You can't let your fears get the best of you.''

"But, Murray, this is only a one-story building. Do you want to go over to the top of Sal's building next? It's two stories.''

Murray walked over to where the ladder met the building and grabbed Jack's arm. "Let's not push our luck. Help me get offa here.''

Jack stepped on the ladder and held a hand out to Murray who swung on like a pro.

As they were backing down, Jack had another question. "Murray, what are you really afraid of, not just the black cats and ladder stuff?''

"It already happened, Jack. When my Eva was killed the worst fear at the darkest place you can go inside your mind happened right before my eyes. After a thing like that, you know anything is possible.''

"Are you still afraid?''

"Of everything, Jack, of everything.''

TWENTY

"ARE we stopping to pick up Bo?" Joe asked. He could see the Texan waving to them from a parking lot ahead.

"No," Heaven answered. "But maybe Bo will ride with us. We're stopping here because we have to. Passenger cars aren't allowed at Maroon Bells during the summer. It's an environmental thing. We park here at the T-Lazy-Seven Ranch and get a ride in a horse-drawn wagon. Normal tourists would have to take a bus in from town."

"Thank God we're not normal tourists," Chris said smugly and started to get out of the car.

"Wait," Heaven commanded. "Do we know what we're supposed to do?"

"Talk to as many of the nominees as we can, one on one," the boys recited, rolling their eyes.

Heaven caught the eye-rolling. "There's something going on. You know it and I know it. Don't act like I'm being hysterical."

Chris tried to soothe her. "We're just giving you a hard time."

Heaven didn't even acknowledge Chris's attempt at niceness. "I doubt if Ernest will be here, but everyone else will probably show. Try to get them to talk about the mishaps."

"Whoever set this up is a pretty smooth cookie. If it is

one of the Best Chefs I doubt they'll spill their guts if we lean on them,'' Joe pointed out.

Heaven was not to be deterred. "We don't know that for sure. The culprit may be dying to confess to an understanding person. But that's beside the point. Just go out there and nose around and that's an order.''

Bo Morales knocked on the driver's side window. "What's all that whispering? Are you three getting out or did you just drive up here to have a conference in the van?''

Heaven opened the door and Bo caught her hand, kissing it with his usual corny style as she hopped out.

"We came to swill champagne with the finest and fairest. Will you ride up to the party on the wagon with us?''

Bo tucked Heaven's arm in his and headed for the flatbed wagon that had five or six partygoers on it already. "I was waiting for you. Tab told me you three were a big hit this morning and that you'd be along any minute. He and Ms. Lunch plowed through here forty-five minutes ago. Congratulations.''

Heaven grabbed Bo's hand to steady herself as she climbed up on the wagon. She found a bale of hay at the back of the wagon bed and plopped down. Bo, Joe, and Chris hopped on, along with some winemakers from Bordeaux. Soon the mammoth Belgian work horses plodded ahead and they started up the road to the most photographed peaks in North America, maybe the world. On the way, Heaven pointed out the avalanche runs where tons of snow had tossed hundred-foot pines and stands of aspens like pick-up sticks.

She also showed off a little. "Did you know that aspens, the trees, grow in these big pods? A bunch of related trees have the identical DNA, or whatever tree DNA is called. They are identical clones. A huge batch of aspens somewhere out here in Utah or Idaho is the largest organism in the world. Cool, huh? You know how a bunch of aspens will turn yellow in the fall, but some right next to them won't? If they're right next to each other you'd think they would have the same weather conditions and turn fall colors at the same time, but they don't. They turn fall colors when their family, their organism, all turns. How do you think they communicate with each other? Isn't it mind boggling? A whole mountain full of trees thinking as one.''

"How do you know all this?'' Chris asked skeptically.

"I've been to the Bells before and gone on hikes with the Mounties.''

"I bet you have,'' Joe chimed in.

"I mean the state conservation people. Forest rangers. Lots of them are women.'' Heaven defended herself with a kick to Joe's leg. He laughed and moved out of range.

Bo was leaning back against a bale of hay. He had black leather chaps on, black jeans, a black gingham shirt with a gathered yoke and black suspenders. Heaven couldn't look in his direction. He tickled her cheek with a piece of straw. "I wish you'd been my science teacher, Heaven. You have a way of explaining things that even makes botany exciting.''

"I'm sure any science teacher would roll their eyes at my explanation, but you get the general idea. Aspens aren't like your run-of-the-mill tree, that's for sure,'' Heaven said dreamily, her mind full of the beauty of the mountains and off the festival troubles for a few minutes.

Soon the wagon came around the final bend and the whole company of partygoers gasped. The breathtaking beauty was enough to do that to anyone, no matter how many times they had visited the spot. Three peaks, South Maroon, North Maroon, and Pyramid, rose majestically in the background. A crystal-clear lake shimmered in the foreground. The lake was nestled in a wide valley so it was possible to hike around the lake on gentle slopes before you had to begin any serious climbing. And in this beautiful valley, the Champagne Council had added some manmade delights that made the scene almost surreal.

In a meadow full of wild flowers, a hot-air balloon was tethered. Three black-and-white-striped tents were looped with garlands of flowers, greenery, and colored ribbons. They

looked like the movie set of a medieval jousting tourney. A
Parisian street band was playing gypsy music; violins pierced
the air with passionate melodies. T-Lazy-7, the guest ranch
nearby, had brought horses for guests to ride up to a nearby
waterfall. A uniformed state conservationist was conducting
a hike. Down by the lake a fly-fishing instructor was teaching
several people how to cast a fly rod. It looked like a nature
version of Disneyland for adults.

To top it all off, the moment they jumped off the wagon,
a lovely French woman was there with a bottle of Laurent-
Perrier and a glass.

The quartet looked around at the elegance, the scenery, the
opulence. Joe let out a low whistle.

"I think this is the time to use that old stand-by line,"
Heaven said quietly. "Joe and Chris, we're not in Kansas
anymore."

"If anyone can use that old standby, it's us," Chris said.
"Let's eat."

Bo pressed Heaven's hand. "I think I'll go down and
check out the fly-fishing. See you in a minute."

Heaven spotted Rowland down at the lake, rod in hand.
"There's Rowland, getting tangled in his line. I wonder if
they have trout in Australia," she mused.

Heaven, Chris, and Joe headed toward the tents. They
walked in through a doorlike opening. It looked like a salon
at Versailles, brocade couches and chairs, thick rugs, silk
pillows, the works. Behind or in front of each sofa or chair
was a trained massage therapist, rubbing heads, necks, hands,
and feet.

Heaven threw her hand up to her forehead in mock disgust.
"I should say we need a massage. What with the drinking
and the eating and the drinking and the eating, I'm just a
tense, nervous wreck. This is the most decadent thing I've
seen in my years of coming to the festival. I love it."

"Well, we are tense, nervous wrecks and we do deserve
a head rub," Chris said. "After all we've been through, what

with Sergio, Tony, and Ernest all in danger of extinction. But can we eat first?"

"My thought exactly. I'm starved. We didn't have breakfast, did we?" Heaven asked as they hurried into the food tent.

The lunch was a perfect French country spread, or at least what the French thought the foodies of America would want to eat.

There was a huge tray of every pâté made in France, many with truffles and foie gras. There were cheeses that someone must have smuggled in the country in their suitcase—they certainly didn't look like the pasteurized versions of French cheese that were legal in the United States. There were huge round galettes and quiches and tarts with Swiss chard and goat cheese and onions and Gruyere and ham. There was a cold lentil salad, eggs in aspic, smoked trout mousse, a chafing dish with escargot redolent with garlic and Pernod.

A team of chefs were cooking crepes to order and the variety of fillings to put in the crepes was staggering, anything from creamed chicken to caramelized pears. Even Nutella, that jarred hazelnut goo that is so much a part of the Paris sidewalk crepe stand, was available. Bread had been flown in from Pouilane, the famous Parisian baker. French pastries took up their own huge round table. Heaven loaded her plate. Chris and Joe each had three plates, one just for sweets. They found an empty table outside in the sun and claimed it. A cool breeze was fluttering the garlands of flowers and ribbons. People were speaking French. It was just like in the movies.

"I feel like a greedy child," Heaven happily murmured with her mouth full. "Pouilane bread and good cheese would be enough. But I had to have some onion tart and a crepe and the lentils are so good. They must be those little ones from Puey."

Lentil Salad

1 lb. green lentils
1 cup walnut oil
⅓ cup tarragon vinegar
1 T. Dijon mustard
1 red onion, diced
1 shallot, finely minced
Options: walnuts, feta cheese, cucumbers, celery

Try to find the green French lentils but the brown ones will do. The red lentils get too soft for this salad. Cover the lentils with water, bring to a boil, then reduce heat and simmer until tender, about 30 minutes. Check often at the end so the lentils don't get mushy. Drain and rinse. Transfer to a mixing bowl and add the diced red onion. In a separate bowl, mix the shallot, mustard and vinegar together. Slowly add the oil, whisking the dressing as you add the oil to emulsify. Toasted walnuts and feta are great added to this salad, but a diced cuke or two or three stalks of celery sliced have far fewer calories.

Goat Cheese Tart

1–2 cups caramelized onions
1–2 cups goat cheese
⅓ cup Parmesan cheese
8 eggs
½ cup cream
2 T. water
nutmeg, kosher salt, white pepper, sugar
olive oil and butter
9-inch pie crust, pricked with a fork and par-baked five
    minutes at 350 degrees

How to caramelize onions: Peel, split, and slice four large sweet onions, placing the cut side of each half down on the cutting board and slicing very thin. In a medium sauté pan, melt 2 T. butter and combine with 2 T. olive oil. Add the onions and when they are soft and beginning to look translucent, then add 1 T. kosher salt and 1 T. sugar. Toss the onions with the seasonings and continue to cook over low heat. Stir every five or ten minutes and let the onions turn a soft brown or caramel color.

In the prepared pie crust, place the onions, as thick as you want them. Crumble goat cheese on top of the onions. Make a custard by beating the eggs and combining them with the cream and water. Season with salt, pepper, and a dash of nutmeg. Pour the custard over the cheese and onions. Top with Parmesan and bake about 45 minutes at 350 degrees, or until the custard has set and a knife comes out clean from the middle of the tart.

Just then, a server made the rounds with more champagne, this time Tattinger. Heaven took a drink and looked around. "I see Linda Lunch and Sergio, over on the other side of the lake. I wonder what those two have to say to each other that they had to move out of eavesdropping range?"

"Stop detecting for just a minute and enjoy the moment," Chris ordered. "Look, here comes Tab."

Soon their table was crowded as Tab and Rowland and Bo all found their way to this spot in the sun.

Heaven looked around at her friends. She felt her throat tightening up. "I'm such a wimp. I feel so happy to be here right now that I'm . . ."

Joe grabbed his napkin and wadded it up, aiming for Heaven's head, but not actually throwing it. "No tears. If life is ever perfect, it's now. Don't start blubbering on us."

Bo wiped his mouth after finishing off a petit four that looked to be constructed out of pure butter-cream frosting.

"Every nominee has a reserved table tonight. Since I don't have an entourage of fans, I'd be honored if you would sit at my table. Me and Mercedes and my brother will come out and sit down after my course is served."

Rowland shook Bo's hand across the crowded table. "A reserved table is a real treat. It can get hectic in there when the foodies and winos all rush the ballroom. Thanks."

After three desserts, a crepe with Nutella, a meringue shell filled with fruit and a baby crème brûlée, Heaven finally remembered her mission. She excused herself from the full and lazy crew and went over to the pastry table where Lola Castro was standing alone.

Heaven introduced herself with a smile. "I'm Heaven Lee, from Kansas City."

"I'm Lola Castro."

Heaven grinned. "A little nervous about the dinner tonight?"

Lola shook her head. "Not really. I've had a life full of adventures, Heaven. This is just one more, if I win or if I don't. But I am more than a little concerned about the accident rate of the Best Chef candidates. I want to get back to Miami in one piece. I didn't escape from my fifth cousin Fidel to die in this paradise."

Heaven looked at the woman beside her. She had salt-and-pepper hair held back in a French braid, a handsome face and beautiful bronze skin. She looked about sixty. Heaven's instinct told her that Lola wouldn't stoop to dirty tricks to win this contest or anything else. Of course, Heaven knew she was susceptible to women with hardship in their past but who had made their own luck. It was a blind spot. "I wondered if you were related. You must have some stories to tell. I'm sure nothing else will happen, Lola. After all, we only have a few hours to go. Good luck tonight," Heaven said warmly as she turned back to her table in the sun.

The troops were finally rousing from the stupor of champagne and pâté. Chris pointed at the hot-air balloon. "The nice lady that brings the bubbly around said Dom Perignon was being served on the ascent. Why don't you see how the world looks from there, H? Bo is going to try to show Tab and me how to fly-fish.''

"Bo is a brave man," Heaven retorted. "Where's Joe?"

"He thought he spotted Tony La Sala and took off at a breakneck speed," Chris answered.

Heaven started toward the balloon, but when she saw Sergio and Linda Lunch in line for the scenic ride, her amble turned into a jog of sorts. Upon reaching the line, two women stood between Heaven and her prey. Heaven put on her most convincing sweet face. "Do you think I could cut in front of you? I have to leave in twenty minutes and I goofed around at the food tent. I was saving the best till last and I guess I just saved a little too long. Please?"

The two women were not thrilled, but they let Heaven move in front of them. The balloon was almost down to earth.

The idea seemed to be for three or four people to hop in the basket and ride the balloon to the end of its tether, drinking a glass of one of the world's most expensive champagnes and surveying the stunning scenery, then coming back to the ground. Because they were deep in conversation, Linda and Sergio didn't notice who was hopping in the basket with them and the pilot until lift-off. Linda Lunch was not pleased to see Heaven.

"Sergio, Linda," Heaven said brightly. "Another beautiful day in paradise, eh?"

"Heaven, what in the hell happened last night with Ernest?" Linda snarled, ignoring the niceties.

"You know as much as I do, Linda. I think Ernest needs a driver for the rest of the trip."

Sergio poured both the women Dom in fresh glasses. He shook his head at Heaven. "You were almost run down by a drunk Cajun. I hear you also had a run-in with my son Tony last night. You and the pastry chef from Washington. Trouble seems to follow you, Heaven. I am grateful, however, that it led you to find me the other morning. I haven't thanked you for whatever you might have done." Sergio bowed slightly in Heaven's direction and waved his arm toward the mountains. "All these petty mishaps pale in importance up here in the air, don't you both agree?"

Linda Lunch narrowed her eyes. Heaven would not have been surprised if a forked tongue had darted from Linda's mouth as she looked with irritation at Sergio. "Sergio, can the sweet talk. You always were the worst bullshitter I ever . . ." She broke off the sentence and turned to glare at Heaven.

Heaven saw an unfinished sentence hanging in the air and went right for it, even though she was a little nervous about their increasing altitude. She didn't think survival was an option from this height if Linda suddenly pitched her over the edge of the balloon basket. "You said you *always* were to Sergio, Linda. Are you and Sergio old enough friends to have an *always*?" She let the implication lie there for a minute before she smiled sweetly.

Sergio leaned over and rested his arms on the rail of the basket, looking out. He answered for Linda. "When I first came to this country, I went right to San Francisco. I worked everywhere, the Fisherman's Wharf seafood houses, the hotels, some French restaurants because that was considered the epitome at the time. My cookbook came out then and Linda worked for a San Francisco magazine as the restaurant reviewer. She did a story about my book. Have I thanked you for that story lately, Linda?"

"Not since 1971, asshole," Linda snapped, and was sorry for being so hateful the minute the words came out of her mouth. He was trying to give her a compliment and she had called him an asshole for his efforts.

Sergio looked over at Linda, who studiously avoided the surprised gaze of both he and Heaven by feigning interest in the sights.

"Was your wife from Italy as well?" Heaven asked.

Sergio's face clouded over. "Yes."

Heaven couldn't stop now. "And Tony was born in San Francisco?"

"No, Italy. My wife was pregnant when I got my first job offer in the States. She wanted to stay in Lucca to have the baby. Both of our families were there, so I went off without her. She died in childbirth. When Tony was old enough to travel I insisted he come be with me. It was the only part of his mother I would ever have." Sergio looked genuinely sad. Linda choked on her champagne and coughed loudly for a minute. Sergio patted Linda's back until she jerked away. When her coughing spell was over, Sergio added, "Of course, Tony is a U.S. citizen now."

Heaven's mind was racing. Did Sergio hate Tony because his birth had killed Sergio's bride? What about Linda and Sergio maybe having an affair when Sergio was alone in San Fran? Did Linda choke because Sergio was speaking fondly about his dead wife?

Linda cleared her throat one more time and took a shot at Sergio. "Too bad you didn't leave the little bastard over there. He's been a royal pain in the butt for you, Sergie."

The balloon was descending. Heaven tried to steer the conversation away from the argument Linda seemed determined to pick with Sergio. "I have a feeling everything bad has already happened, and that the chef's dinner tonight is going to be a huge success. Good luck, Sergio." With that, she hopped out of the wicker basket.

Tony La Sala was lurking close to the balloon and Heaven marched right for him. She couldn't tell if he was trying to get his father's attention or trying to hide from Sergio's sight line.

"Well, Heaven. Are you going to throw more food on me today?" the churlish young man asked, not looking smart enough to be nervous around Heaven.

"Interesting man, your father," Heaven began, choosing to ignore the allusion to the night before. "He was telling me about your mother and about how he went to the new world to seek his fortune. I'm sorry about your mother's death.''

"It's all just a fairy tale to me. I never knew my mother, of course. And my dad never wanted us to visit her relatives in the old country. His parents lived with us a few years when I was in high school. Couldn't even speak English. They were old and sick. My mothers were the restaurant bookkeeper and the waitresses and girlfriends along the way. My dad was the guy on the cover of a book. Chefs don't make good parents, but you know that. You have a kid.''

"Touché, Tony. Iris, my daughter, never felt . . .''

"Oh, that's right. I remember the story from my time in Kansas City. You didn't start cooking until you couldn't be a lawyer anymore. I guess your daughter just had to worry about you going to jail.''

"I can't believe I felt sorry for you just a minute ago. Your pitiful motherless childhood got to me. I hope your sauce curdles tonight, Tony,'' Heaven said as she hurried away. Her face was pounding with blood. She wanted to throttle him but she knew her lurid past was fair game. As she rushed toward the departing wagon dock, she ran smack into Joe and Chris, almost knocking Chris over.

"Whoa, missy. How was your ride in *Around the World in Eighty Days*?'' Chris queried as he held Heaven's arm for a few seconds. He could feel her trembling.

"Very informative. Linda and Sergio knew each other way back when in San Francisco. Way before Sergio's wife had arrived from Italy, which she never did because she died when Tony was born.''

"Is that what made you so angry?'' Chris was concerned.

"Oh, no, Sergio's rotten kid did that, not the circumstances of his birth. Can we go?''

Joe stepped in and took Heaven's arm conspiratorially. "You and I are going home for a nice nap. Chris is going to stay out here with Tab until everyone is put on the wagons and the last bottle is put in the recycling bin. You have to take everything out that you bring in.''

Chris looked like a teenager asking permission to stay out after curfew. "Tab and I want to hike up by the waterfall. I promise I'll be home by five, in plenty of time to change. I know I can't ask you to not tell Joe any news until I get home. Just promise you'll tell me what I missed."

Heaven patted Chris's arm distractedly. "Have fun. Where are . . .?"

Joe led her away, glancing back at Chris with a tiny bit of worry in his eyes, for Heaven, not Chris. She had certainly fixated on this Best Chef problem. "Bo had to go, he was revved up about tonight, said he had to go work on the fire. Rowland went off with some Italians. Said he'd meet us at the hotel at eight."

Heaven looked at her watch. "It's only two. We have time."

TWENTY-ONE

"WHAT happened to the nap idea?" Joe whined.

"That was your nap idea, not mine. Go around the block. I'm just going down this alley to check it out. I'll be right back," Heaven said as she slipped out of the passenger side of the van.

They were looking down a service entrance of the Hotel Jerome. Joe had serious reservations about this course of action, but hadn't been able to talk Heaven out of it. He pulled away as ordered. Sure enough, two minutes later Joe was back from a trip around the block and Heaven was back from her recon mission. She jumped in the van without looking behind her.

"I can't believe I'm the wheel man on this heist," Joe said as he turned onto Main.

Heaven pulled a crumpled piece of paper out of her bra. "Ta-da! I didn't even have to break into Ernest's car. The car door was standing open. I think one of Ernest's cousins must have been unloading their food."

Joe pulled over to the curb and put the van in park. "First, I can't believe Ernest's car was still road-worthy after last night. I guess that stump wasn't as big as it seemed last night. Second, I don't believe you found the note and didn't get caught by those monster cousin boys. You live a charmed life, boss."

"The note was folded neatly on the dash. I think Ernest was going to show it to the police to try to prove his story. I guess we could return it to him later. Now, go out of town the way we went last night. I'll navigate with Mindy's map."

"You don't really think there is a Mindy, do you? Or that she'd give him her own address or phone number?" Joe asked rather nervously.

"Probably not," Heaven conceded. "But if she thought he didn't have a chance of arriving, who knows? It may have been easier to draw a map to her own house. A woman who gets paid to slip someone a mickey can't be that bright. I'm sure the name and the number are wrong. Did you see who Ernest was talking to last night at the bar?"

"With the scene you played at the bar, who had time to keep track of Ernest?"

"I didn't pay enough attention either. I do remember him coming in the bar and I vaguely remember someone blond beside him but that's it. Who knew it would be important later?"

As Joe and Heaven made their way over the rising curves, Joe glanced sideways at Heaven. "I'm sorry."

Heaven took off the reading glasses she had put on to figure out the map. "About?"

"Tony and his nasty remark about Iris. I'm glad you finally told me what he said. I could tell you were upset."

"Yes, I was. But not half as upset as I would be if Tony was my son." Her smart crack broke the tension and the two laughed. All of a sudden Heaven pointed and yelled, "Turn here."

After two more twists and another turn, two small log cabins came into view. A pick-up truck and Honda stood in the shared drive. Just at that moment, a blond woman came out of the door of one of the houses, heading for a clothesline in the backyard.

Joe gave Heaven a high five. "What can I say? She's a dumb blonde who used her own house on the map," he chortled. He quickly pulled the van in the driveway. As

Heaven opened the door, the woman saw them. Her reaction was immediate. She ran for the house.

Heaven jumped out and ran for the door of the house. She was closer to the door than the blonde and put out her hand like a traffic cop when the woman approached.

"We're not the cops. We're not Ernest's loved ones. We just want to ask you about last night. We'll pay," Heaven added as extra incentive, although she wasn't sure how much cash they had on them.

The blonde was young, dressed in cutoff jeans and a tight T-shirt. Her huge breasts stood too alert to be natural. Her face would pass for pretty only in a dimly lit bar. In daylight she looked young and vacant, with eyes too small and lips too big. "I don't want any trouble," she said. "I just heard from a friend of mine in town that one of the chefs from the festival had a car accident last night. I knew before she told me it was Ernest. I feel just terrible. If he had been hurt or killed . . ." Her voice trailed off.

"Are you a dancer?" Heaven asked.

The blonde looked down shyly. "Yeah, down in the valley at the Relay Station. Someone called there and asked for a girl to entertain one of the chefs. Said he was real shy and they wanted to give me to him as a little gift. But then, it got complicated."

Joe spoke up. "They asked you to drug him?"

"Not exactly . . . well, sorta. But they said they wanted to make sure he passed out, had a real bad hangover today. They said they would fix up a hot toddy that would make him feel real sick in the morning. I picked up my money and a flask of the booze I was supposed to give him from a bartender I know at the Tippler. They said I had to be sure he drank some before we left town, that he would just fall asleep and never make it out of the parking lot. They also insisted I spill some of it on the car seat. I figured it was someone who wanted the hometown boy, Tony La Sala, to win. It sounded harmless enough at the time. I'm really sorry. Are the cops going to come?"

Heaven held up the map. "I'm surprised they haven't been here. Not too smart to use your real location, Mindy. Is it really Mindy?"

"Barbara. Actually, it was a house down in the valley. I guess you didn't follow my drawing too well."

"We were lucky you came out to get your wash when you did," Joe said. "You may be lucky too. This map may have been under the seat or hidden somewhere in the car when the cops towed Ernest's car. Ernest may not have had time to mention you to them. But he had the map all straightened out and sitting on the dash. I think taking it to the police was his first order of business after the big dinner tonight. We just borrowed it for the afternoon."

Heaven went in for the kill. "Barbara, I assume you never met the mystery man or woman who hired you?"

"No, just like I said. A phone call and then an envelope with the cash, the flask, and instructions, very James Bond. I kind of got a kick out of it, you know, be at the Cavern Club at eight. Ernest Laveau is thirty-eight, brown hair and beard, beer belly, the only one with a heavy Louisiana accent."

"Speaking of accents," Heaven chimed in, "how did this person sound over the phone?"

"That's funny," Barbara said. "I hadn't thought of it until now, but he had one too."

"One what?" Joe and Heaven said more or less at the same time.

"An accent. But his wasn't Cajun, like Ernest."

"British?"

"Spanish?"

"No, Southern. He was young, a man with a thick Southern accent."

Heaven and Joe looked at each other. Heaven held out the childishly drawn map. "I can't think of any good that will be served by the police seeing this or by Ernest and his cousins finding you. This is better than cash, Barbara. Say thank you."

"Oh my God. Thank you so much. I am so thankful for this," she dangled the map gingerly between two fingers, "and that Mr. Laveau wasn't hurt."

As Heaven and Joe headed for the van, Heaven said over her shoulder to Barbara, "Don't come to Aspen until Monday afternoon." She didn't know what Ernest would do if he spotted Barbara/Mindy. It wouldn't be pretty, Heaven knew that much.

Tab Garner opened the door to his hotel room and glanced hopefully at the phone. Thank goodness the message light wasn't blinking. He had to have a minute to take a shower. Relaxing was out of the question, but twenty minutes without Linda's voice, which had become more shrill as the festival progressed, was essential to getting through the evening.

As he stood in the shower, Tab thought about Chris Snyder. They had been able to enjoy an hour alone at the Bells, hiking to the falls. Chris was a pleasant surprise. They really got along. For a minute, Tab let his mind drift. He could see it now, Tab Garner, not just art director but executive editor of *Foodies* magazine with his life partner Chris Snyder, famous playwright. He saw them in their Tribeca loft. He could picture the piece in *New York* magazine, or better yet, in the *New York Observer*. The shower ran out of hot water and Tab came back to the present.

Tab had invested in a Ralph Lauren tuxedo last year. As he put it on, his confidence returned. He looked great in a tux.

The chefs' accidents had thrown him for a loop. Add to that what the mishaps had done to Linda and the result was a very stressful situation. Tab had lost his inner calm on Thursday night at the Little Nell bar and it hadn't returned. The Best Chef dinner was just a couple of hours away. It would all be over soon.

Tab picked up the phone and dialed. "Hi. Let's get started so we can get this over with."

*   *   *

Linda Lunch threw the Vera Wang across the room. Tonight, only Chanel would do. She'd wear the pink boucle Chanel suit with the Chanel belt of the season, the gold one that cost $1200. There were enough people in Aspen who would know a $1200 Chanel belt when they saw it to make a statement. The belt would say Linda Lunch was still in control.

She didn't even mind the rumors that she was behind all the unfortunate incidents with the chefs. It was better for them to think that she was a vindictive bitch than having people believe someone could invade her turf and destroy her event.

She'd find out who was really responsible for all these attacks when she got back to New York, she was sure of that. Then, whomever it was would be crushed. This morning she'd thought she'd seen the food editor from *Gourmet* at the Ritz having breakfast. When she'd marched into the dining room for a confrontation, it had turned out to be a festival attendee from Omaha. If only she had more time. She needed to set some records straight, do some housekeeping when she got back to New York.

Linda checked her makeup for a final time. The whitish pall, the pall that she liked, had been replaced with a pink glow. "Damn the French. They would have to have their picnic outside in the sun," she muttered to her image in the mirror. She quickly found the Chanel powder and remedied the situation.

Two more bruises had popped out on Linda's body, one barely showing on her neck above the collar of the suit. She used the powder there too. Then she took the pills out of a small bag and looked at the labels. "Two of these and three of these. And how long will they work? Not long enough," she said as she swallowed them down.

Linda opened and shut the door to her hotel room twice, the last time slamming it forcefully. "This is ridiculous. I've made up my mind. There's no turning back now," she muttered. Linda picked up the phone and dialed quickly from memory, even though she had never called the telephone number before.

"This is Linda. We've got to talk. No, it can't wait until after the dinner. Now."

Murray looked around the empty dining room. Every table had a clean black tablecloth covered with white butcher paper. The bistro glass full of colored markers on every table was full of fresh markers. One of the things people liked about the cafe was the chance to be artistic. Everyone drew pictures on the butcher paper with the markers. Heaven insisted they provide markers instead of crayons because the markers' brighter colors made better table-top art. The markers also cost twice as much as crayons but Heaven wouldn't switch just to save money.

Murray had been on top of the world all day. He felt like he had slain a dragon by climbing up that ladder. After his therapy session with Jumpin' Jack, he had gone for breakfast, walked forty-five minutes in Loose Park, and come back to the restaurant about two in the afternoon to piddle around. He changed the tablecloths, even though the busboys could have done it later. He filled the markers because it was fun. He'd even drawn a picture on the butcher paper, a cartoon of Jack and Murray on the roof.

The cafe wasn't open for lunch on Saturday. He had expected Heaven to call and he was ready to confess everything about the Auto Club inspectors and Jack but she hadn't called yet. He glanced at his watch. It was four-thirty. All of a sudden, Sara Baxter appeared in the dining room.

"Murray, have you ever worked the grill station of a busy restaurant on Saturday night?" Sara asked.

"Me? I'm a mean man on the grill. I can do a burger that makes 'em weep. But I don't do Saturday nights. I'm more of a Sunday afternoon-type griller."

Sara grimaced. "Well, I think you just got promoted. I cut myself." She pulled her right hand from behind her back. It was wrapped in two kitchen towels that were red with blood.

Murray felt queasy but he didn't want to let Sara down. After his triumph on the roof this morning he couldn't let a little blood bring him back to his former wimpy state. "Do you need stitches?"

Sara sat down at the nearest chair. Her skin was gray. "I think so. Will you take me over to the med center? We sure have been good customers this week."

Murray took Sara gently by the arm. He tried to sound jovial. "That was Heaven's idea. She didn't want Hank to have any time off while she was out of town. I hope Hank is in the emergency room now. Come on, let's go. On the way you can tell me about the grill station."

Sara smiled weakly. "I was just kidding about the grill. I think you'd do better on salads and desserts. I know hand cuts, Murray, and I know I won't be back at work tonight. But I'll be fine by Monday, I'm sure."

"Whatever it takes, Sara. We've had a rooftop rescue, an Auto Club inspection team, and a Jumpin' Jack attack. Surely after all that, I can make a few salads. I'll ask the bartenders to watch the door. Let's go," Murray said bravely.

"You'll be wishing you were back up on that roof after a Saturday night in the kitchen of Cafe Heaven," Sara said as they walked out the door.

TWENTY-TWO

THE ballroom and front dining rooms of the Hotel Jerome were full. There were even tables set up in the lobby. Six hundred and fifty excited diners were finding their seats and their friends.

Heaven was sitting at Bo's reserved table, pouting and enduring a lecture from Joe. Joe had sent Rowland and Chris off on a wild goose chase to find Tab. Although he knew perfectly well that Tab was across the room by the bar, he had suggested Rowland and Chris look in the lobby.

"Pay attention, little missy. Your lip curled visibly when Tab's name came up. You better get a hold of yourself. I thought we made a deal. We said we are not going to tell Chris tonight that we suspect his new flame is a mole in Linda's backyard, or a traitor. We'll tell him tomorrow. After all, what could it hurt for Chris to have a nice time tonight?" Joe scolded.

"I know, I know. But it just makes me want to puke when Chris goes on about what a great guy Tab is, what fun they had hiking the Bells. Yuk."

"You liked him a few hours ago. And he isn't the only man in the world with a Southern accent, H. Probably not the only man in Aspen with one either."

"Just a little too much of a coincidence for my liking, Joe. You agreed it was a major break in the case."

"And you agreed nothing could be done tonight, so why spoil the evening? On Monday we'll go back to Kansas City and Tab will go back to New York. So far everyone has been sent to the hospital, not the morgue. If it stays like that, we can put it in the win column."

"OK, OK," Heaven said but it didn't stop her. "I wouldn't put it past Linda to order Tab to play the dirty tricks. She's sneakier than Tab, that's for sure. But why would she want to sabotage her own festival? Then, there's the possibility that Tab is sabotaging it for someone else. Then, there's the third possibility, that Tab has his own agenda."

"I can't stop your wild imagination, but please don't let your suspicions show. Can you be cool?" Joe asked as he pinched Heaven's cheek.

Heaven kissed Joe on his hand. "As a cucumber."

Rowland Alexander returned to the table and again sat down next to Heaven. "Chris found Tab. By the way, Heaven, you look great tonight. You too, Joe."

Heaven, Chris, and Joe all wore vintage tuxedo jackets, the guys with jeans and tux shirts, no ties. Heaven had on something that looked like a cross between a bodysuit and a bustier, with tux pants and Italian high heels. She had piled her hair up in a loose French twist and finished the whole look off with the tux jacket and some antique garnet earrings. She batted her eyes at Rowland. If nailing Tab to the wall as suspect number one was out of the question tonight, she'd just have to flirt. "Why thank you for noticing. I can hardly wait for dinner. I wonder who drew the first course?"

When the nominees for Best Chef were announced in April, a phone lottery gave each chef a course for the big dinner. The order was kept secret until the very moment of presentation. Which was now. Half of the serving staff walked formally into the ballroom with menu cards which they passed out as the second half brought out bowls of steaming soup.

"Great," Heaven said, throwing down her menu card,

"Tony La Sala has the first course. I'll be sick to my stomach for the rest of the night."

Tab and Chris rushed to their seats. "What have we missed?" Chris asked.

Joe looked across the room. "Not a thing yet. The first course is on the way at this very minute. Says here: Tony La Sala, Cavern Club, Aspen, Colorado. Potato soup with mushroom broth, truffles, and Parmesan. Wine: Domaine Chandon Reserve, Brut, NV."

As the soup was served, Heaven couldn't resist a little interrogation. "Tab, where were you hiding?"

Tab looked miserable. He glanced over at Chris who quickly took up his slack. "Tab is a little worried, H. Linda Lunch hasn't shown up at her own party."

"You're kidding," Heaven said, feeling a chill go down her spine. "Did you look in the kitchen? Maybe she's back there making the cooks cry. This is great sparkling wine by the way."

Tab sipped the wine and shook his head. "She's not there. I've never even beat Linda to the dining room before. She's usually down here at five, driving everyone crazy."

"What about her room? Maybe she fell asleep or just fell," Joe offered.

Tab shook again. "I had a manager open the door with a passkey, which would have been a death sentence if she'd been in there. She wasn't."

Suddenly the table was lulled into silence by the smells emanating from the soup bowls in front of them. Enough sliced truffles to choke a horse were sitting on top of a mound of potato puree infused with truffle oil. Around the potatoes a broth laden with wild mushrooms floated like a moat. Curls of Parmesan cheese topped the dish.

Truffled Potato and Mushroom Soup

    1 lb. red potatoes or Yukon Gold potatoes, peeled and
      boiled until tender

2 turnips, peeled, quartered and boiled along with the
   potatoes (The turnips will take a little longer to cook
   so either put them in the boiling water first or leave
   them in longer when the potatoes are tender)
1 lb. assorted exotic mushrooms: shitakes, crimini, mo-
   rel, porcini, etc.
2 oz. dried porcini mushrooms, soaked in warm water
   for at least an hour
shaved Parmesan cheese, as good as you can afford
1 qt. chicken stock or vegetable stock
truffle oil and truffles (You can do without the truffles
   but you need to spring for the smallest bottle of truffle oil you can find)
cream
olive oil
butter
kosher salt, white pepper, and freshly ground pepper

Heat 2 cups cream and 3 T. butter and mash the
potatoes and turnips together, adding the cream/butter
mixture a little at a time until it is creamy. Different
potatoes absorb moisture differently so you have to
stop adding liquid at the consistency you like. Season
with salt and white pepper, and add the truffle oil a
drizzle at a time until the truffle aroma permeates the
mixture.

Slowly sauté the mushrooms in equal parts butter
and olive oil (usually about 2 T. each). Add the stock
and the reconstituted porcini. You can use the broth
from the soaking of the dried mushrooms also but be
careful to add it in slowly and not use the dredges,
which can be sandy. Heat through.

To serve, spoon a helping of the potato/turnips in
the middle of a heated soup bowl. Surround with the
mushroom broth. Top with shavings of Parmesan and,
if it's in the budget, thinly sliced truffles.

"And they called this mere potato soup. Tony has never been the modest type before. This is stupendous," Chris admitted grudgingly.

Heaven jumped out of her chair as if she were on a spring. "I knew it! He's done it again. This isn't Tony's dish. It's Todd English's from Boston. He made it at Charlie Trotter's in Chicago for a James Beard dinner last year. I'm telling."

Tab looked alarmed. "Now, Heaven, even if you're right, and I'm sure you are, what are you going to do? Go to each table and tell them what a recipe thief Tony La Sala is? That would take a week. We're just going to have to trust that one of the other nominees does a better job and wins the award."

Rowland looked around at the nearby tables. "It was delicious. People are groaning with pleasure."

Heaven looked down at her empty soup plate. "It was great, just like the last time I ate it. Come on, Bo, baby. Our hopes and dreams rest with you." She stood up. "I'll be right back," she said.

Tab looked worried. "Heaven, you won't commandeer the microphone and tell everyone about the soup, will you? Linda would have a fit."

"Trust me," Heaven called over her shoulder. Her choice of words made Chris and Joe look worried too.

Heaven wanted to check the ladies' room. The large powder room near the ballroom was full, but she blundered in and quickly opened or peeked over the five stalls with a "So sorry" after each invasion. No one familiar. She made a pass at the front desk, asking if they had seen or heard from Ms. Lunch. Nothing. Heaven arrived back to the table just in time for the second course.

As the server passed out the collector menu cards, each course card nicely designed by a different Aspen artist, he made a little bow towards Heaven and pointed at the card. "You are mentioned, Ms. Lee," he said, proud of recognizing her.

This course was that of Bo Morales, Triple M Ranch, Amarillo, Texas. The card read: Slow-smoked and grilled sea-food with a trio of sauces: the Triple M Ranch sauce, Heaven Lee's Royal Jelly, and Barbara Tropp's Sesame, Soy, and Plum sauce, in honor of these two women who are present tonight. Wine: Bert Simon Kaseler Kehrnagel Spatlese.

Shrimp in the Shell

1 lb. colossal size shrimp, or as big as you can afford
½ cup orange juice
½ cup rice wine vinegar
⅓ cup molasses
2 T. soy sauce
1 T. sesame oil
1 tsp. Worcestershire sauce
1 tsp. five-spice powder
1 chopped jalapeño
juice of one lime

Combine all of the ingredients and toss over the un-peeled shrimp. Let marinate for at least an hour and up to eight hours. In other words, you could put the marinade on in the morning and cook the shrimp in the evening. Cook shrimp directly over hot coals about five inches above the fire if you have a choice. Cook 3–4 minutes on each side and watch them closely, removing them when the meat turns opaque.

Heat the marinade to boiling and simmer five minutes or so, until it has reduced and thickened slightly. Pour over the shrimp after you take them off the grill.

If you aren't in an outdoor grill mode, heat a dry sauté pan. When the surface of the pan is radiating heat, sprinkle 1 tsp. kosher salt in the pan and add the shrimp. Cook 3 minutes or so and then turn the shrimp over and add some of the marinade to the hot pan. The shrimp will take five or six minutes to cook. If you

have to use smaller shrimp, it will take less cooking
time. This indoor method works very well but it is
smoky, so open a window or door before you begin
the process. The shrimp end up a deep caramel color.
Don't forget to suck the shells.

Heaven blushed. She was genuinely touched. Even though
she knew Bo was playing her like a bluegrass fiddle, she
couldn't help falling for it.

The servers emerged from the side doors holding a small
Weber grill for each table. While one server removed the lid
of the little Webers, the other put plates in front of each diner
with puddles of the three sauces: a tomato-based sauce with
pepper and other spices floating in it; that one was Bo's;
Heaven's was a golden color, and Barbara's a deeper soy
and plum mauve.

The grills on each table were obviously just for show.
They were too clean to have been used. Each grill contained
two or three coals still giving off enough heat to keep the
food warm. The food was being served, not cooked, in them.

The assortment of sea treats was tantalizing. Roasted oysters with their tops popped open from the heat gave off the
aroma of the sea. Next to the oysters lay a whole smoked
Coho salmon. Next to the salmon were slices of rare grilled
tuna charred with a crust of peppercorns. Around the rim of
the brazier, huge grilled prawns, heads on, were perched,
marinated and glistening brown.

On every table were baskets of those cornbread muffins
with the cracklings baked in them. Heaven had to hand it to
Bo. This family-style serving method had sure loosened up
the room. Even the food snobs were laughing and grabbing
prawns with their bare hands. Everyone at Heaven's table
was excited.

"Try the oyster with Bo's sauce. It's very New Orleans."

"How did he get the tuna to taste smoked and still be
rare?"

"Your sauce is great, Heaven. What's the fruit?"

Heaven tried to answer with her mouth full. "Pickled peaches. I gave Bo the recipe last year." She swallowed an oyster and washed it down with a gulp of wine. "This is a tour de force. In one course, Bo shows slow-cooking with the salmon, marinating with the shrimp, grilling with the oysters, and at least two techniques that I can't figure out with the tuna. I hope the crowd appreciates the skill involved. And fruity German wine really shows off the food, too."

Joe patted her hand. "You know what Bo would say, you have to educate the public. And the public seems to be having a ball."

Heaven looked around. The noise level had gone up several decibels during the barbecue course. Usually the room wasn't this loud until after the entree. As Heaven got up, so did Tab.

"I have to go check with the manager," Tab muttered.

Heaven let him get a head start, then she made a dash for the stairs. During the oysters, she decided on linen closets as her search project for this break. She could just see Linda tied up with a gag in her mouth, lying in the bottom of the dirty linen hamper. She laughed to herself at that mental image as she headed up to the second floor. She certainly didn't trust Tab to do all the searching alone. Not after what Barbara, aka Mindy, had told them about a man with a Southern accent. By the time she poked her head in the last closet on the fourth floor, she had jumped to another disturbing conclusion.

Maybe the person responsible didn't have a Southern accent at all. Suppose someone had paid Barbara to say that a man with a Southern accent sent her? They only had the word of a topless dancer, someone who was willing to slip some stranger a mickey. Maybe the whole episode was a plot to make Tab look guilty. Heaven trudged down the stairs, empty-handed.

It was time for the entree. Bo, his brother, and sister-in-law were already seated, looking relieved to be done with their part of the evening. Before Heaven sat down, she wrapped her arms around Bo and his chair and gave him a big kiss on the neck. He caught her by the arm and kept her close for a second too long, nuzzling her hair a little with his lips.

Heaven straightened up, breathless and at least four degrees warmer than before. "Good job, friend. You brought the spirit of barbecue to this uptight event. Everyone is more relaxed, thanks to you." With that, she slipped into her chair, trying not to pant out loud from her encounter with Bo or her four-story dash up and down hotel corridors.

"Heaven, where did you rush off to?" Tab asked suspiciously.

"I had this brilliant idea that Linda might be locked in a linen closet, so I took a look."

"In all of them?" Joe asked.

"Lucky there are only four floors in this hotel. If we were in New York I'd be screwed," Heaven said.

The next menu card read: Sergio La Sala, Sergio's, San Francisco, California. Venison in the manner of Lucca on porcini risotto cakes, squash blossoms, and Barolo reduction. Wine: La Scarpa Barolo.

Sergio's Venison

venison tenderloin, or in a pinch, pork or beef tenderloin
olive oil
butter
onions
chicken or veal stock
red wine
red wine vinegar
3 cloves garlic
cloves, parsley, bay leaves, thyme, kosher salt, sugar, black peppercorns
½ cup white raisins
½ cup lightly toasted pine nuts

Anyone from Lucca already knows that Sergio's dish is not from that town. This recipe is adapted from a rabbit dish from Sicily. The sweet and sour elements go really well with game. I've made this with elk tenderloin as well as deer.

For the marinade: Combine 2 cups red wine, 1 onion sliced, chopped parsley, 3 cloves garlic, 3 cloves and 6 peppercorns smashed with the flat side of a cleaver, 2 bay leaves crumbled, 3 sprigs thyme. Heat this just to a boil, cool down to warm and pour over the meat in a bowl. Refrigerate and marinate for at least two hours; overnight is better.

Roast the tenderloin in a hot oven, 450 degrees, approximately 20–25 minutes. The length of time will depend on the size of the tenderloin and the desired doneness.

Heat 2 T. oil and 2 T. butter in a large heavy sauté pan. Add 1 onion, diced and sautéed until it is light brown. Then add the marinade liquid and 1 cup stock and simmer to reduce. In a small heavy pan, slowly melt ⅓ cup sugar. When it turns golden brown, add ½ cup red wine vinegar to the sugar, stirring constantly with a wooden spoon. Add the raisins and cook a minute, then add this mixture to the sauce. Add pine nuts at the last minute and pour over the tenderloin, with extra sauce in a bowl for spooning.

This dish is good served with creamy polenta, creamy or stiff risotto, flat noodles like fettucine, or mashed potatoes.

Squash Blossom Risotto

1 medium onion
2 cups Arborio rice
3 cups liquid, beef, vegetable, or chicken stock, or wine

butter, kosher salt, white pepper
Parmesan cheese
olive oil
eggs
bread crumbs
mozzarella cheese
squash blossoms
Options: You can substitute squash blossoms with
  mushrooms or leftover meat or chicken

The idea of this dish is to cook the risotto until it's three quarters done, then quickly spread it out on a greased baking sheet to cool down. At this point the rice is refrigerated so it is stiff. This makes it easy to work with to form patties and the like.

Sauté the diced onion in 3 T. olive oil. When the onion is translucent, add the rice and coat with the oil. Start adding broth ½ cup at a time, stirring often with a wooden spoon. When all the liquid has been absorbed, quickly add 1 T. butter, salt and white pepper, ½ cup Parmesan and spread on your prepared baking sheet. Add squash blossoms (or mushrooms, or leftover meat or chicken) to the risotto mix at this point. Chill.

You can make risotto patties by hand with the chilled rice, adding a slice of mozzarella cheese in the middle of the patty. Or you can use a biscuit cutter, cut triangles, or even use a star cookie cutter. First dust the rice cakes with flour. Second, dip your rice cakes in an egg wash made of 3 eggs and a little cream or milk. Then dip them in bread crumbs and sauté them in a mixture of butter and olive oil at a medium heat. They will become brown and crispy.

You can use these cakes as the base for a meat course, as Sergio did, or serve them with sautéed mushrooms, black beans, or summer vegetables as a terrific meatless main course.

As the plates arrived, everyone oohed and aahed. The stiff risotto cakes formed the base for a tower of food, but not a contrived tower, a tower that seemed organic and made perfect sense. Resting on the crispy round of rice was a filet of venison, topped by a soft mound of sautéd squash blossoms. One perfect zucchini blossom had been fried in a light beer batter and seemed to be growing out of the top. An intense red wine sauce was drizzled around the plate and studded with raisins and pine nuts.

"What's Lucca style?" Bo asked before he disturbed the masterpiece with his fork and knife.

"I think it's with raisins, pine nuts, and balsamic vinegar," Heaven answered as she rotated her plate to admire the design. "No wonder Sergio has outlasted most of his peers and is still going strong. I wonder where he got the squash blossoms?"

"I heard in the kitchen that he had them flown in this afternoon from Santa Fe," Bo said. "They came from Elizabeth Berry, the famous organic farmer. They were picked this morning."

Everyone nodded, mouths full. For a few minutes, the table was quiet in appreciation of a master's work.

Rowland spoke only after devouring every morsel on his plate. Heaven loved that about him. He could eat. "I've never really understood the voting process, Bo."

Bo smiled. "It's simple. Everyone votes on each dish, giving it a score of one to ten, ten being the highest. The vote is not relative to the other courses. If you think they are all tens, then you give them all tens. After the whole meal is finished you rate each course one to five, according to how it rated with the others. The chef with the highest score on the final vote wins. The best single course, sometimes it's the same as the best overall, sometimes not, gets the *Real Dish* award, which is different from the Best Chef award. *The Real Dish* prize is a trip to wherever the chef wants to go for food, education, or inspiration."

Heaven was interested. "Where would you go, Bo?"

"India to learn about cooking with tandoors. It's the opposite of slow cooking at low temperatures. It's fast cooking in hot earthenware ovens at eight or nine hundred degrees."

As Tab excused himself again for another conference with the banquet manager, the rest of the table settled into convivial small talk. But Heaven was scanning the room like a secret service agent. She was lucky enough to spot Tony La Sala slinking out of the ballroom, looking furtively from side to side. Heaven got up. This was the best break of the evening.

Heaven had no idea where Tony was headed, but something in his manner made her think it wasn't the men's room. By the time she exited the ballroom he was nowhere in sight. She made a quick visual sweep of the crowded hallway and decided it was time to check out the kitchen. Suddenly a loud crash erupted from the other side of the door Heaven was just about to enter. Voices started yelling in Spanish and English. There was a loud whooshing noise which sounded like water.

Most older hotels have a large, central kitchen that serves all departments. The banquet preparations, the line cooking for the dining rooms and the room service all are generated from the same prep areas and storage spaces. Heaven didn't know exactly where the Best Chef cooks were headquartered, but she pushed open the main kitchen door and found pandemonium.

The fire extinguishing system had obviously gone off, pouring water and chemical foam all over the kitchen. A kitchen worker had apparently slipped in the mess and dropped a load of plates, which now lay broken all over the floor. The hotel chef was screaming at his team, trying to determine if there really was a fire. The air crackled with tension, but seemed smoke-free.

In the middle of all this madness stood Lola Castro. She was bent over a long table, trying to shield the food laid out in front of her. She had not been successful. The baking sheets were loaded with tiny, filled pastries, which Heaven assumed were empanadas, rows of round fritters, and salad plates loaded with tiny baby lettuces. Everything was swimming in an inch of water and covered with thick white foam. Lola Castro was crying.

Heaven touched her arm gently. "It's a good thing this didn't happen to one of the men. They wouldn't know how to make a silk purse out of a sow's ear like we do. Now, take a deep breath."

"I just know there isn't any fire. Someone did this to ruin me," Lola cried, wiping her eyes with the tail of her apron.

Heaven pushed a loose strand of hair back from Lola's face. "Well, then we can't let that happen. Tell me what the dishes were and then we'll figure out an alternative."

Lola looked down at the soggy mess in front of her. Her chin quivered. "Baby greens topped with an empanada filled with Cabreles cheese. When you cut into the empanada, the hot blue cheese runs over the greens. Baskets of yucca fritters. Passion flower dressing." Lola brightened up. "The dressing is still in the walk-in," she said. "The plantain chips might also be safe. We made them this afternoon and stored them in airtight containers. Someone went to get them in the pastry room. The pastry room was probably flooded too."

"It sounds wonderful." Heaven waved at one of the hotel cooks. "Can you get us the porter?" she yelled across the chaos. "And the chef?"

One of Lola's team from Miami came back to her side with a big smile on his face. "The plantains are OK."

The good news was the turning point for Lola Castro. That and the sight of Sergio La Sala and Ernest Laveau striding across the kitchen to help. "We're here," Sergio said simply. Ernest just started instructing the kitchen crew to remove the remains of Lola's course.

Soon the porter and chef were by Heaven's side. She took charge. "Look, I know you have a mess here, but we also have six hundred people that probably don't know that a disaster just occurred. They are expecting more food. Do you have any jicama?"

The kitchen porter consulted his clipboard. "We should have a whole case."

"Mango? Pineapple?" Heaven asked.

"Sure do."

"I saw two more wheels of Cabreles in the walk-in," Sergio said. "I'll get a crew busy wedging it up."

The hotel chef was motioning to his employees. "We can clean up later. Let's get this course out the door first. Get all the mango, pineapple, and jicama out of the walk-in. Get the salad plates cleaned and cooled. And I'll go see if there is enough spring mix or spinach."

Lola put her arm around Heaven and gave a little squeeze. "But the course will be late going out to the dining room. It'll take twenty-five minutes at least to create a new half-ass dish."

Heaven slipped off her tux jacket as a hotel cook passed aprons and chef coats around to the extra help. "They hadn't started pulling the plates when I left the dining room. Everyone needs a break anyway. You did them a favor. I'll peel the jicama. I'm a champ at it. I'll need a couple other people to cut it into strips."

"What can I do, Lola?" It was Bo Morales, at Heaven's side. "I knew by the look on the waiters' faces that something had gone wrong," he explained. "But the front of the house is happy. They're just starting to clear the last course."

Lola looked at Heaven for direction. Heaven grabbed six workers looking for jobs and pointed at Bo. "Take those cases of pineapple, peel them and cut them into rings for Bo to grill."

The chef came back shaking his head. "Not enough lettuce or spinach."

Lola was suddenly back in control. "That's OK. I think I see the plate now. Heaven, will you keep everyone working while I experiment?"

The next thirty minutes were the most focused the hundred or so people in that kitchen had ever experienced. Brigades of food people worked side by side, hands and fingers flying.

The end result probably wouldn't win Lola Castro the Best Chef award, but it wouldn't put her to shame either.

A grilled slice of pineapple was topped by a chunk of Cabreles cheese. Slender sticks of jicama and mango were arranged artfully to give height to the plate. The plate was drizzled with Lola's special passion flower dressing which added an intense color. Two or three plantain chips were stuck on the top of the cheese as the final touch.

Passion Flower Dressing

⅓ cup passion fruit nectar (Good substitution: Dole makes two juice blends with passion fruit in them, a tropical fruit and a passion-banana-pineapple)

2 passion fruits, peeled and seeded (Good substitution: 1 mango, peeled and sliced)

⅓ cup white vinegar

⅓ cup lightly toasted sunflower seeds

⅔ cup sunflower seed oil

1 tsp. kosher salt

Put everything but the oil in the food processor and turn on. Drizzle in the oil to emulsify. You can throw in an additional handful of sunflower seeds right before using. This dressing is good with a salad of greens, goat cheese, and berries and also great on a grilled chicken breast.

When the last tray left the kitchen, the entire ensemble broke into applause. Lola started to thank everyone, but Heaven stopped her, "You're not done yet. I want you to take off your apron and go and tell everyone what happened. When they see what's in front of them, they'll know you're a magician. Now get."

Lola hadn't survived a hostile takeover of her country to be defeated by a kitchen disaster. She was ready to save her reputation with the foodies. She took off her apron and blew a kiss at the crew. ''I owe you all one, big time,'' she said as she strode out to the ballroom.

TWENTY-THREE

HEAVEN turned to Ernest Laveau. "Did any of your food get spoiled? Do you need us to help?"

"No, I was lucky. All my stuff is in the pastry room or the freezer. And I've got the boys working right now." He turned to the kitchen crew. "Don't forget me when it's time for dessert. I'll need help plating this damn thing. I've got hot and cold on the same plate."

"Heaven, shall we join our party?" Bo asked.

Sergio gave Heaven a peck on the cheek. "I'm going back to join mine. Good work, you two." He shook Bo's hand and left the kitchen.

Heaven was strung as tight as Christmas tree lights. She couldn't sit down yet. "I'll be right out. I'm just going to hit the ladies' room first."

Bo smiled. "Food people always pull together. Everyone but Tony, I guess."

Heaven hadn't seen Tony since he slunk out of the dining room. It didn't surprise her that he hadn't come to help, but where was he? Of course, he could be sitting at his table right now, enjoying the pain that Lola Castro was going through. Heaven hoped he was at his table. At least he would be accounted for.

"Bo, screw Tony and the donkey he rode in on. He's no help in a jam, take it from someone who knows. However,

I'm sure glad your sixth sense sent you to the rescue. I'll see you in a minute," Heaven said and headed in the direction of the kitchen bathroom. She remembered where it was, but had no intention of using it. She took a look up and down the hallway. No one was paying any attention to her. She was just another person in a chef's coat at this point. She opened the first metal door she came to and stepped in.

"Meat and fish walk-in," she said out loud. Heaven poked through the fish and shrimp, moving a couple of pans and looking behind them. She didn't know what she was looking for. She opened the door, stepped back out in the hall and moved to the next metal door.

"Prepared foods and produce, second door," Heaven recited. This refrigerator unit was much bigger. There were cases of oranges, apples, and lettuce stacked on pallets. Stainless steel baker's racks were loaded with clear plastic containers holding a variety of salads. Sliced turkey and ham and pastrami were in half pans ready for sandwich making. Heaven picked up a slice of turkey and absently ate it as she looked behind and below things like she was on a kitchen scavenger hunt. A few minutes later, she leaned on a door release knob and pushed through the door. Walk-ins were designed for people with both hands full.

"Door number three," Heaven said as she entered what turned out to be the freezer. It was huge, Aspen being not exactly on the beaten path of food delivery. Heaven assumed the hotel bought frozen things in large quantity so a blizzard wouldn't close the dining rooms. That's the only thing that would justify all these frozen products. There was a rack and roll, which was a series of shelves with wheels, stacked with baking sheets full of glass plates that already had praline candy cups full of ice cream. Heaven delicately picked up a scoop of the ice cream and took a pinch off of the bottom and stuck it in her mouth, then put the ice cream back. "Banana with chocolate chips. Delicious," she murmured.

As Heaven moved back in the vast room, she bumped into a wooden pallet stacked high with boxes of tiger shrimp.

There was an insulated blanket thrown over the whole tower of shrimp and Heaven grabbed at it to maintain her footing. Her high heels, hardly safety shoes for the kitchen, slipped again on a small patch of ice and Heaven started to go down, the blanket still in her hand. As she fell, something wrapped up in the silvery quilting of the blanket hit her. It was Linda Lunch.

Heaven landed on her butt, legs splayed in front of her. She looked down at Linda. Linda looked up at her, eyes staring vacantly, her head at a right angle to the rest of her body. There were ugly marks on her throat. It looked like Linda's scrawny neck just hadn't stood up to the torment. Heaven gingerly touched Linda's arm. It was hard to the touch but not completely stiff. Heaven shuddered. All of a sudden she realized where she was. "I better get out of here or we'll both be frozen stiff, Ms. Lunch," Heaven said as she slipped out from under the blanket and got up to her feet, leaving Linda wrapped up like a baby.

Heaven was a little wobbly, but she hit the door with her full weight, anxious to get out and get help. The door didn't budge. She threw herself at the door again. Nothing. A moment of panic fell on Heaven. She pounded and screamed, knowing that the chances of someone hearing her from the other end of the hall were nil. "Take a deep breath," Heaven ordered herself aloud. She turned back toward Linda's body and saw the rack and roll with Ernest's dessert in front of her.

Heaven checked her watch. "Thank God. Ol' Ern will have to come for his ice cream in ten minutes or so. I'll be fine." She walked carefully past the shrimp and spotted a canvas jacket hanging on a hook on the back wall.

"The poor sucker who has to inventory this place must leave this in here. Thank you, brother," Heaven muttered as she slipped it on. She blew on her hands and knelt down beside Linda Lunch. "We'll be out of here in a few minutes, Linda. Just try to stay limber a little longer. What happened, babe? Did you get in someone's face once too often?"

Heaven spotted the bruise on Linda's arm. One of Linda's hands showed a purplish spot as well. "Whoever did this to you seems to want to do the same thing to me, or at least the flash frozen part. But ol' Ern will save me, I hope."

To make the time pass, Heaven got up and went through the shelves. "Puff pastry, spanakopita, peas, squid. What variety. Boy, Linda, is Ern going to be pissed to have you upstage his dessert course. And this is really going to throw a damper on the Best Chef contest." Heaven realized how true that would be. The contest would screech to a halt. The whole festival would be ruined. She stared down at the body wrapped in the blanket and let out a big sigh.

Heaven took her shoes off and hopped around on the cold floor in her stocking feet. She couldn't fall again. She lifted the blanket and tilted Linda back on top of the cases of shrimp. The body flipped over facedown. "Say thank you, Linda. Ernest was a good guy and helped Lola out. And you would just shit if you ruined your own party. So just stay put, honey. I'll be back for you as soon as dessert is over."

Heaven turned Linda over on her back and carefully covered her with the insulated blanket, walking around the pallet to make sure that no hands or feet were sticking out. "I'm glad you're a ninety-eight-pound weakling, Linda. We'd be out of luck if you were my size," she puffed.

Noise in the hall sent Heaven over to the door. "Help. Help. I'm locked in here," she yelled at the top of her lungs. "Ernest!"

Cursing ensued. Heaven could hear Ernest and the cousins out in the hall, talking to each other in Cajun dialect. The sound of metal on metal was followed by the swinging of the walk-in door. Heaven threw herself in Ernest's arms.

"You were locked in, my praline cups were locked in with ya, missy. What happened?"

"I'm not sure." Heaven's goal was to get the Louisiana team out of the freezer before they accidentally spotted Linda. She grabbed one of the rack and rolls with Ernest's desserts, threw off the jacket and tried to hustle the whole crew out the door. On the way out, she looked at the door. "I guess this freezer has an outside lock so everyone can't help themselves to the shrimp." Bad choice of words, she thought as she hurried them down the hall. "It must have accidentally locked on me."

"Like I accidentally drugged myself and drove that car purt' near in the river," Ernest grumbled. "I'll be so glad to hit the Louisiana state line I can taste it. Let's get this show on the road so we can leave this God-forsaken place."

Heaven helped them get the ice cream to their station. She found her tux jacket and traded in the kitchen apparel. "I'm going into the dining room and enjoy whatever you're going to do with that praline cup. The ice cream is great. I sneaked a taste."

"Heaven," Ernest roared as she turned away, "be careful."

Moments later, Heaven was back at her table. She told the story of the fire extinguisher and the freezer in her usual amusing way. Joe and Chris didn't believe she was telling the whole story for a minute.

"So you just happened into the big walk-in freezer and the door just happened to get locked?" Joe asked dryly.

Heaven smiled brightly. "Obviously nothing bad happened 'cause here I am. And while I was in the freezer I got a glimpse of our dessert. It looks great."

Bo wasn't going for Heaven's story either. He kept quiet though and just stared at her. He noticed her hands shaking. Rowland watched Bo watch Heaven and he too picked up on her trembling hands.

Heaven listened to the table chat and laugh, but an image of Linda's body was superimposed in her mind, as the rest of the room still enjoyed life.

The menu cards were presented again. Ernest Laveau, Marie Laveau's, Houma, Louisiana. Praline bananas Foster with caramel bread pudding and banana/chocolate chip ice cream. The waiters brought out the plates with the ice cream and bread pudding. Chafing dishes with the bananas and sauce were lit and poured on the ice cream tableside, as the lights were lowered for a dramatic effect. Heaven saw her spoon come to her lips, but she didn't really taste anything. She ate woodenly, agreed that it was a wonderful, fresh version of a group of old favorites.

Ernest's Bread Pudding

1 loaf Italian unseeded or French bread, torn in chunks
brown sugar
white sugar
pecan halves
vanilla extract
cinnamon
butter
4 eggs
1 qt. half-and-half
bananas, one for each person
banana liqueur
rum or bourbon
vanilla or banana ice cream

PUDDING: Melt 4 T. butter and ½ cup brown sugar together until the mixture is bubbling. Line the bottom of a greased round cake pan, individual custard cups or a springform pan with most of this, leaving a couple of tablespoons for later. Add pecan halves to the brown sugar, in a circular pattern if you want.

Make a custard with the eggs, half-and-half, 1 T. vanilla, and 1 cup white sugar. Add the remaining butter and brown sugar to this to flavor it. In a large bowl, soak the bread in the custard for twenty minutes before placing in your baking dish or dishes. Break up the bread a little more as it becomes soft. When you pour the bread and egg mixture in the baking dish, it should still be very wet. Add more half-and-half if this is not the case. Bake at 350 degrees until it is set and the middle is firm. Let cool to warm before inverting and serving.

BANANAS FOSTER: For each serving, melt 1 T. butter and 2 T. brown sugar in a heavy sauté pan or a chafing dish. Slice and add 1 banana and a dash of cinnamon to the butter and sugar and sauté until bubbly. Add ½ oz. of banana liqueur and your choice of rum or bourbon and flame. Serve with a wedge or individual serving of the bread pudding, a dip of ice cream and the bananas poured on top.

As the waiters brought coffee and offered cognac, she looked anxiously around the room. The servers were starting to collect the voting ballots.

Once more Heaven got up. The whole table groaned.

"Where this time, Heaven?" Tab asked. "I've already looked for her in the men's room."

Heaven leaned in towards the table slightly. "No one move. I have something important to tell you, but I have to do one thing first. I promise I'll be right back," she said and then headed for the front desk. She tried to talk herself into just telling the manager where to find the body and letting him or her do the rest. But she had discovered Linda and it didn't seem right to just casually announce, "Oh, by the way, the missing editor is in the freezer with a broken neck, go get her."

Heaven asked to see the manager on duty, pacing around the front desk until she appeared, which was only two or three minutes, but seemed an eternity.

The manager was an attractive woman in her fifties, dressed in her best power suit for the special occasion. She looked at Heaven expectantly. "Can I be of help?" she asked.

"We have to call the police and have them meet us in the freezer. Linda Lunch is in there and she's dead."

TWENTY-FOUR

THE light in the ballroom was dim. Joe and Chris had refused to leave Heaven alone at the hotel. The three of them were sitting around a bare table in an empty room. After a few hours, they had finally persuaded Rowland and Bo to go home. Tab was still around somewhere. Heaven was drinking from a rather full glass of cognac. Joe and Chris had made coffee, drunk it, and started on beers an hour ago. It was two in the morning.

"So, go ahead," Chris urged. "What did the investigations officer say then?"

Heaven rubbed her head. "He said he guessed I knew I should have reported the body as soon as I found it. He asked why did I move the body. I said I didn't move the body on purpose, or at least the first time it wasn't on purpose. I said of course I knew about reporting a dead body. I'd made a judgment call about letting the dinner continue. I said if I ever found another body in Aspen I would call him immediately. He wasn't amused. I imagine having to process more than seven hundred people who contaminated the scene of a murder would make you lose your sense of humor."

Chris attempted logic. "Actually, probably only the hundred or so people behind the scenes could have actually gone to the freezer."

"The place was a madhouse," Heaven reminded them, "and no one was watching that hallway."

Joe rubbed Heaven's neck. "So can you leave now?"

"I think so. I'll just check with Investigations Officer Kent Rainey, who must be sick of seeing me every day." Heaven got up and took another gulp of cognac. "This has been a long night. Chris, where's Tab?"

The three of them walked toward the kitchen, where clean-up and interrogation were both being concluded. Chris looked around hopefully. "I'll try to find him to say good-bye. He took this whole thing very hard," he said and headed for the lobby.

"As bitchy as Linda was, I'm sure it was still a shock. If your favorite horrible boss dies, who do you complain about?" Heaven asked absently.

Joe looked across at Heaven sharply. What would he do if something happened to Heaven? He was sure someone had locked her in the freezer earlier, even if she didn't want to admit it yet. There were so many angles to this case. His mind raced to Mindy who was really Barbara, and the Southern accent they thought was Tab's. Right now Tab was either feeling very guilty or very grief-stricken.

As Joe and Heaven hit the almost empty kitchen, Investigations Officer Rainey was deep in conversation with a kitchen worker. Tears were running down the young man's cheeks. Rainey looked up sharply at Heaven, then said something in Spanish to the young man. He nodded yes to the officer, they shook hands, and the man walked away, wiping his eyes with the back of his hand.

"Is anything wrong?" Heaven asked. "Of course, lots of things are wrong, but is anything new wrong?"

The officer looked around the room. "Have you seen Mr. Garner lately?"

Heaven felt fear for the second time in the same evening. She hoped Chris didn't find Tab. "Chris, my friend, went to locate him. I haven't seen Tab for some time. Why?"

"The young man I was just talking to confessed that

someone paid him to pull the kitchen fire alarm tonight. He was very upset. He was afraid his actions had somehow contributed to Ms. Lunch's death. Five hundred dollars is quite a bit of money. Five hundred dollars just to pull a switch.''

"What does that have to do with Tab Garner?" Heaven asked.

The officer continued. "This fellow says that the man who hired him told him the payoff money would be in the freezer, under a case of frozen peas. He picked up the envelope with the money in the freezer about five, the time the voice on the phone said it would be there. He didn't meet his new employer, never saw him, but he did have one clue to pass along.''

"A man's voice with a Southern accent?" Joe and Heaven said more or less at the same time.

Before the officer could ask them how they knew, Chris Snyder came into the kitchen. "I looked for Tab, even went up and knocked on his door, but there was no answer. No one has seen him for at least an hour.''

Heaven had to ask. "Was the body—was Linda—already in the freezer when the guy picked up the money?"

Officer Rainey shook his head. "Of course, the kid says it wasn't. And we'll know more when the Pitkin County coroner does his thing. But I don't think Ms. Lunch had been in the freezer that long. That freezer has a temperature of zero degrees. If she had been in there since five, I think she would have been frozen harder by the time you found her at ten or ten-fifteen. I thought perhaps the kitchen mess was to create a diversion so the killer could move the body to the freezer, but again, the rigidity isn't right. The only thing we really know is that the person who sabotaged the dinner was familiar with the freezer and knew there were frozen peas in there. Now how did you know about the Southern accent?"

Chris looked at Heaven and Joe with alarm. Heaven put up her hand in a stop gesture to prevent further questions. "Just a lucky guess. There are lots of Southern accents at this festival. Why, three of the five chef nominees are from below the Mason–Dixon line. We're leaving now, officer, if we may.''

"Be careful, Ms. Lee," Officer Rainey said solemnly.

Heaven turned and saw the look on Chris's face. The look said he had lots of questions. It was going to be a long ride up the mountain. But just when she had given up hope of the night ever ending, Chris came through like a champ.

"Lucy, you've got some 'splainin' to do," he quipped in his best Desi Arnaz accent. Then he switched back to Chris. "I can tell you know something I don't. But I don't want to know until morning. We've had enough. Let's just go home.''

TWENTY-FIVE

WHEN Murray finally walked out into the dining room after his first Saturday night shift as a pantry person, he got a standing ovation. Of course, only the staff remained in the cafe. The customers had gone home to bed. But Sam, the bartenders, and a couple of the other servers were still there, doing their checkouts and having a beer. They cheered Murray's debut.

"Those Blue Heaven salads were beautiful tonight, Murray."

"You did a great job on the brownie sundaes."

"You were slow as molasses, but you were better than nothing."

Murray smiled and took a little bow. "I don't drink, but if I did I could sure use a drink right now. I have a whole new respect for the kitchen. My feet are killing me."

The front door opened and in came Jumpin' Jack and Hank, Heaven's boyfriend.

Murray plopped down on a bar stool and started untying his shoelaces. "What are you two up to? Coming in to see what new disasters have occurred?"

Hank put his hand on Murray's arm. "Don't do it. Take it from someone who spent fifteen hours on their feet today. If you take off your shoes, you'll never get them back on to drive home. Just tough it out a few more minutes."

Murray looked wistfully at his tennis shoes. "It's warm out. If I have to drive home in my bare feet, it won't kill me." He took off both his shoes and his socks. "Oh, dear God. That feels so good. I don't know how you do it, Hank. Of course, you're much younger."

Hank and Jack had taken stools on either side of Murray. "My feet aren't young. Doing your residency gives you very old feet. Can we still get a beer?"

One of the bartenders nodded from down the bar where he was sitting and dealing with his credit card slips. He quickly poured two Boulevard Beers, the local Kansas City brew. He also gave Murray a large glass of Diet Coke, his favorite.

Murray looked from side to side. "So? How was Sara's hand?"

Hank sipped his beer and smiled. "She took a good whack at it, that's for sure. Went down the side of her forefinger and into that soft part where the thumb attaches."

Murray held up his hand. "Stop right there. No more details, please. Stitches?"

"Three," Hank replied. "Jack came down and sat with her. It took about an hour for me to get to her. We were busy early today. A gunshot wound at two in the afternoon."

Murray felt bad. "I'm sorry I just had to dump her in the emergency room. I had to get back and learn my new station in the kitchen. It sure was on-the-job training. Jack, thanks for sitting with Sara. How did you know?"

Jack, so agitated the night before, was as calm as a Buddha tonight. The trip to the roof had been good for both Murray and Jack. "I came by right after you left for the hospital. The kitchen told me what had gone down."

Hank looked over at Jack with a twinkle in his eye. "Yes, and after Sara was sewed up, Jack walked her back to her car down here. Then he came back and sat in the ER lobby the rest of the evening. Said it was fascinating."

Jack looked solemnly over at Murray. "There are lots of sick people, Murray. I really felt sorry for them."

Murray chuckled. "Just last night, Jack my buddy, you could have been a patient yourself. Now here you are, taking care of Sara, feeling bad for all those sick people. What a difference a day makes, eh, Jack?"

"Speaking of a day, has anyone heard from Heaven today?" Hank asked.

Murray shook his head. "No, and I'm surprised. I thought she'd call this afternoon."

"She called yesterday, but I haven't heard today either," Hank said. "I guess there's really no reason to be concerned."

"With Heaven, there usually is reason to be concerned," Jack stated frankly.

"My grandmother used to say 'no news is good news' and maybe . . ." Murray said.

Hank and Jack looked at Murray. "I mean, what could happen?" Murray asked weakly.

Jack answered, "Hospital or jail."

TWENTY-SIX

CHRIS put down the phone. "That was Tab. He wants to see us."

Heaven and Joe looked up from the breakfast table with sleepy concern. It was Sunday morning, about ten. They had just finished confessing to Chris about the Southern accent connections over the pot of Costa Rica Estate Designate coffee, which was a poor substitute for sleep.

On the ride home from the hotel the night before, Joe had asked Heaven to tell them again about finding Linda laid out on the shrimp. They were all so giddy from exhaustion, by the time they got to Peter Cooper's mansion they were laughing as though they had just spent the evening at Comedy Central. Heaven confessed how she had talked to the corpse.

Five hours of sleep found Joe and Heaven groggy but able to tell Chris that Tab was a suspect in their minds and in the minds of the Aspen police.

"You didn't ask him up here today, did you?" Joe asked nervously.

Chris looked miffed. "Please. I've only known this guy three days. If he turns out to be a serial killer, well, I've been wrong before about men. And I've worked on enough investigations to know how to handle these things. Meet in public places. Make sure someone knows where and when the meeting takes place. I'm not just off the turnip truck.''

''Where and when?'' Heaven asked.

''I'm meeting him at eleven at the Weinerstrube,'' Chris said. ''It's one of the locals' favorite breakfast places.''

''At least he's not in jail. Did you ask him where he was last night?'' Joe added.

''He said he talked to the police, then he went to Shooters, which is open until three, then he took a walk. He said he was sorry he didn't let us know he was leaving the hotel, but he just had to get out of there. Blah, blah, blah. His story had more holes than Swiss cheese.''

''We can't figure Tab out now,'' Heaven said. ''Let's wait and hear what the little creep has to say. The awards presentation starts at one. I guess we better get dressed now for the rest of the day. And I, like the fool that I am, invited a movie star to dinner tonight as I recall.''

Joe steered her toward the stairs. ''We'll go grocery shopping later. How hard could it be to cook for us and one movie star? I'm sure she'll just push her food around anyway. We're having breakfast with a criminal and lunch with a bunch of people who must by now wish they were anyplace but Aspen. The movie star is just going to have to take a number to get any attention today.''

Chris looked hurt. ''Did you just call my ex-potential new boyfriend a criminal?''

Heaven decided to prevent the escalation of this line of questioning. Joe did think Tab was up to no good. So did she. ''Stop it now. Chris, you yourself just said that Tab's story doesn't hold up. You two beat it upstairs and get ready. We now have fifty minutes to walk into the Weinerstrube. That means we have thirty minutes to walk out of here. I have to make a couple of phone calls and then I'll be up. I took my shower last night.''

''Miracles never cease,'' Heaven said as they walked into the Weinerstrube. ''Not only did Tab not fink out on seeing us, he has gotten us a table, which is no mean feat in Aspen on Sunday morning.'' When the young man saw them, he'd tried a smile, but it didn't come off. On Thursday, Tab had been exuberant, full of life. Today he looked frail, shrunken.

Joe rolled his eyes. ''Fink out? Fink out? What decade did fink out originate in? What century?''

Heaven poked him. ''Don't make me laugh. I don't want Tab to think we're going to have fun at this breakfast.''

As they neared the table, Tab motioned to the waitress who poured coffee for the table. ''I know how y'all eat by now so I just ordered us everything, pancakes, eggs, hash browns, the works,'' he said. ''We can put it all in the middle and dig in.''

''So the police didn't throw you in jail,'' Chris said acidly.

''They don't know what I'm about to tell you, or they would have,'' Tab replied. ''They haven't asked for a voice lineup of Southern accents yet. They didn't know the truth about Ernest and the girl until last night so they haven't heard her story. I guess Ernest really unloaded on the investigations officer. Told him he'd make sure no one from Louisiana ever set foot in Aspen again. Heaven, thanks for letting the dinner go on. I know you got chewed out for it, but it sure makes my life easier today. At least we can name the winners and end this nightmare.'' Tab hung his head and held it with both hands.

Heaven saw that Tab was teetering on the edge, but that didn't stop her from leaning on him. ''Listen, you seemed like an OK guy. I was glad to see Chris enjoying your company. But everything has changed dramatically in the last few hours. We are no longer dealing with alarming accidents. We are dealing with death. If you don't give me a very good reason not to, I'm going to find Kent Rainey and tell him to arrest you so everyone can leave town in one piece. Do I make myself clear?''

Tab nodded. ''Crystal. That's why I called you this morn- in' I need your help. Just listen for a minute.''

e waitress arrived with a mountain of food. When she

left, he began to talk. "Two months ago I got a call to interview for a job with another magazine. And eventually they offered me the position. I *was* going to be the new art director for *Foodies*. It was a good step up for me and one that would take years to do at *The Real Dish*, where no one leaves until they are dead or retire. I told the editor over there that I couldn't give my notice until this festival was over. It was one of the biggest things we work on every year and I wouldn't do that to Linda. Or anyone. I was a professional, or so I thought." Tab stopped talking for a minute and took a bite of scrambled eggs. No one else broke the silence. They could see he was about to cry, but they weren't going to help him out.

He went on. "When I got to Aspen there was a call from the *Foodies* office. The executive editor got on the line and told me he needed a favor. He said he was sending someone to Aspen to talk to me, that it was very important to my future and my career. I asked him if the only reason I was hired by *Foodies* was so I could do this favor for them. He said that was ridiculous, that I was hired because I was qualified. However, I could think of this little assignment as a condition of employment. I got the idea."

"What did you do?" Heaven asked impatiently.

"I went to this big secret meeting. It wasn't with anyone from *Foodies*. Some local Aspen thug showed up and laid it on the line. My mission was to scare off the chefs, create the impression that being asked to the Best Chef contest at *The Real Dish* festival was not as desirable as it once had been. I had to do it in a public manner, no calling them with secret threats to kidnap their kids. It had to be dirty, so everyone would know and the reputation of the magazine would be damaged."

"Did you do these dirty tricks yourself?" Chris asked angrily.

"Just the laxative in Tony's wine and I don't regret that a bit. After the way he treated his dad, I wish I'd given him an extra dose. The local guy had already hired someone to trash the tent. I don't believe, I don't want to believe, that Sergio was supposed to get hurt. I think Sergio and the vandal just met by accident, or at least that's what I convinced myself. Then the Ernest thing happened and I realized that he could have been killed. And I had hired the stripper. That's when I saw my whole career going down the tubes." Tab stopped and took a slice out of the stack of pancakes.

Heaven felt tired all of a sudden. People were rotten. "I know what you did to Lola. What were you going to do with Bo?"

Tab gave a slight smile. "We were already doing it. Bo was the only Best Chef nominee who hadn't had an accident. Combine that with the fact that to some people a Texas accent is a Southern accent and the finger is pointed at Bo. He's innocent but he looks guilty."

Chris pushed his plate back and folded his arms over his chest. "What about Linda Lunch?"

"You all have to believe me. I didn't kill her and I don't know who did," Tab replied anxiously. "I loved the broad in a funny way. In fact, I wanted to be her. Last night was easily the worst night of my life. I considered a million different angles. I wondered if I'd been set up, if the whole sabotage thing with the chefs was intended to point to me all along. Then when Linda turns up dead, I'm the most likely suspect. The dirty tricks could have just been part of the con."

Heaven couldn't believe the theory. "Does the editor of *Foodies* have a past with Linda? 'Cause if he doesn't, it's a little extreme to kill someone just to ruin their event. Even in the big, bad world of publishing this must seem a little excessive. Are you sure she didn't find out that you were behind all the messy accidents and fly into a rage? I can see this being a sick accident. She comes at you and you struggle with her. She fights and you grab her around the throat and the next thing you know she's dead. You panic and stuff her in the freezer before the big dinner."

Tab dropped his head into his hands again, the picture of

defeat. "It could have happened that way, I guess. Linda definitely would have tried to kill me if she'd known what a traitor I was. But it didn't happen that way. You have to believe me. The killer is still out there somewhere."

"What do you want from us?" Chris asked coldly. "To say gee, Tab, things sure got out of hand, but it's OK?"

"No, of course not. I know I've blown any chance I might have had with you. I really, I . . . Chris, I had our china pattern picked out in my imagination. I just wanted you three to know the truth. As soon as I get done with today's Best Chef announcement, I'll go to the police and tell them everything I've just told you. My career in publishing will be over. I'll be in jail or back in Mississippi, instead of in an office in the Flatiron building."

"Any ideas who the killer is?" Joe asked. He had been shoveling in the food, not saying a word.

Tab shook his head. "Not a clue. If we were in New York there would probably be plenty of suspects, but here . . ." He looked at his watch and then desperately at his companions. "I have a favor to ask of you."

Chris wasn't able to hide his hurt and disappointment. "You've got a lot of nerve."

"I know I do. Would you dress up in your costumes and help me host this event today? I know it sounds cruel, but the show must go on, and you are theater people. If you played some of your characters and helped announce the winners, it would save the day. At this point in the event, everyone from the magazine thinks it would be best to go ahead and hold the awards party. We know that's certainly what Linda would want."

Heaven looked at the doubtful expressions on the faces of her friends, then she spoke. "Look at it from our point of view, Tab. We're not even sure if you should be walking the streets a free man. If you're the killer and we help you and you get away, we'll be guilty of the worst case of bad judgment in history. And believe me, that's saying something because I've shown very bad judgment in my time. On the other hand, we have all sinned, me the most. I wouldn't be here if people hadn't shown some compassion for me in the past. What do you think, guys? It's not like he's asking us to drive the explosives truck past customs.''

Joe got up from the table and threw some money down. ''Tab, we'll help you if you agree to one of us being with you at all times until this award ceremony is over. It can't be Chris''—he gave his friend a firm look—''so it will be me. Chris, you and Heaven can go get our props.''

Chris opened his mouth to argue, then closed it again. Heaven opened hers to explain why it should be her guarding Tab, but she, too, kept quiet. They had their orders. Go get the props.

Heaven reached across the table, grabbed the collar of Tab's shirt, and pulled him toward her. ''If anything happens to either of these men whom I love like sons, I'll hunt you down and rip your heart out with my bare hands. That's a promise.''

TWENTY-SEVEN

MURRAY'S hands were shaking. He'd been up for hours and it was only ten in the morning. He'd tried the usual thing to calm down, a huge breakfast. This time it was Cheerios, fried corn meal mush, American fries, poached eggs, and several toasted bagels. He was still as wound up as he had been when he woke up at six.

The idea had been there from the moment he jumped out of bed. He tried to remember the last time it had happened but nothing came to mind. It had been so long he didn't even know when he had felt like this. He was pretty sure it was the day his Eva died.

He wanted to write. The whole story was there in his mind, swimming around. Whole phrases, sentences even, appeared and disappeared. Could he give up his precious exile? Would he feel guilty at the pleasure of putting those phrases on paper?

It didn't matter what the consequences. He had to give it a try. Murray had long ago given his computer away, so he fished around in the desk drawer and found a legal pad.

As he sat down with carefully sharpened pencils, he couldn't help himself. He laughed out loud.

TWENTY-EIGHT

NERVOUSLY Chris watched the Silver Queen Ski Gondola cars come into the roundhouse and slow down. The festival crowd was packing every car, two passengers facing up the mountain, two facing down. Everyone seemed to be in high spirits, the murder of Linda Lunch bringing a new level of dangerous excitement to the day's activities. Chris clutched the garment bag and moaned. "Can't I just walk up?"

"If you had started a couple of hours ago you could," Heaven said. "We'll spread our props and stuff out in the gondola car so that we don't have to sit with strangers."

"The way my luck is going, I'll probably throw up," Chris said glumly.

Heaven moved up in the line. "No, that would be my bad luck, not yours. Come on, stop pouting. We'll go up here, do a couple of bits for the folks, give out a couple of awards and split. At this point, I don't care who killed Linda Lunch."

"Then why did you tell me to go work out the routine with Joe while you tried to talk to all the nominees one last time?"

"Just habit, I guess."

The next empty gondola swung their way, the door opening automatically when it entered the roundhouse area. Heaven threw their garment bag and tote filled with wigs onto the back seat, grabbed Chris by the hand and jumped in, refusing to meet the glance of the couple behind them. The attendant looked in at them, getting ready to stuff another couple in the gondola.

"We have to rehearse. We're performing in twenty minutes," Heaven proclaimed like a true diva. The attendant sighed and closed their door.

Chris grabbed the edge of the seat as they left the roundhouse and started a rapid ascent. "How fast does this thing go?" he asked, peering down at the ground receding below.

"Something like three thousand feet in fourteen minutes, I think. It's really fun when you go over the first peak. You can't see the village anymore then."

"You call that fun? Trapped on the wrong side of the mountain, probably with a killer," Chris grumbled.

"What do you really think? Tab didn't kill Linda, did he?" Heaven asked.

"I really think I'll never have another boyfriend, that's what I think," Chris said pitifully.

Heaven patted his leg, gazing out the window. They were directly over a particularly deep trench. She had to keep Chris talking. "Stop feeling sorry for yourself. I tried to be skeptical, but I believe the guy. I don't think he would have confessed the dirty tricks if he'd done the murder. And when he was telling us about the dirty tricks, he seemed genuinely miserable."

"He could be miserable and also be the killer. But, I agree with you. I don't think he killed his boss. Can we get down now?" Chris said, eyeing the ground below.

Heaven pointed cheerfully toward the ground. "Now look. The ground is probably only twenty-five or thirty feet down. That's not so bad."

"Yeah, but look up ahead." The gondola was preparing to dangle over a ski run named Silver Dip with the dramatic drop in terrain the name implied. But Heaven didn't mention the name to Chris.

"I think I'll try to find Lola first. She was pretty shaken

by everything that happened last night." Heaven was pretty good at changing the subject but Chris continued to stare earthward as the ground fell off and the gondola rose higher.

She pulled on his sleeve quickly. "Look over there. That's the hip restaurant, Bonnie's, where Donald and Ivana Trump had their big fight over Marla way back when," Heaven said pointing at a building to their right on the mountain.

This bit of Aspen trivia brightened Chris considerably. "How do you get there?"

"You ski down the mountain and stop there for lunch. A couple that used to live in Kansas City owns it."

Chris hugged Heaven's arm. "You're a good baby-sitter. I totally forgot to be afraid. I wonder how Joe's baby-sitting detail is going."

"We'll soon know," Heaven said as the door automatically opened. Heaven reached in the back and grabbed the garment bag. Chris got the tote and they jumped out, absorbing the splendor around them.

Soon Heaven and Chris saw the first wine table and Joe. He was talking to Rowland and they both had something white in their glasses.

Heaven pecked both Joe and Rowland on the cheek and kept walking. "You guys figure out what we're going to do. I'll meet you over at the stage," she said over her shoulder.

Chris looked expectantly at Joe. "How's Tab?"

"Busy. I personally did the ribbon markers. These New York guys thought the setting was enough decor. I told them we had to lead to camera left or we'd lose the crowd to the cafe. Let's go over to the food table. I'm starved."

"How could you be hungry? You ate all the food on our table this morning. The rest of us sensitive types were too upset to eat. Rowland, will you join us?"

"No, lads. I have to stay here and pour some of this delicious Australian Chardonnay/Semillion blend. I'll see you up at the stage at one. Be careful. Heads up."

Heaven was scouring the crowd for a nominee. She saw

Lola Castro and Ernest Laveau and decided to talk to Lola first.

"How are you this morning, or afternoon, I guess it is? I feel like it's all still part of last night," Heaven said as she surveyed the food table and Lola at the same time. The woman looked as weary as Heaven felt. "What's good?"

The table was another example of the bounty that the world brought to Aspen. The Food and Wine of Italy had supplied fresh mozzarella, aged Parmesan and Asiago and crusty breads. They had also hired a caterer to produce an array of frittatas, those Italian baked egg casseroles filled with pasta, vegetables, and spicy sausage.

Pasta Frittata

    2 cups cooked noodles or other pasta
    6 eggs
    ½ cup Asiago cheese, grated
    1 cup ricotta cheese
    olive oil, kosher salt, and pepper
    Options: diced and blanched asparagus, roasted red
        pepper strips, crumbled and browned Italian sausage,
        roasted garlic cloves, sautéed onion

Heat 2 T. olive oil in a sauté pan. Brown the noodles so they have a little color and crunch to them. If you are using long noodles, like spaghetti, cut them into two- or three-inch lengths before frying.

Beat eggs together with 2 T. water, the ricotta, the Asiago, and the seasonings.

In a round ovenproof casserole that you have oiled or otherwise treated (dare I say sprayed with Pam?), layer the noodles and any other ingredients you have decided to include. Pour the egg mixture on the pasta and bake at 375 degrees until the middle is set and the top browned. This should take about 25–30 minutes but will vary with the depth of the baking dish. You can either invert this creation on a platter or cut in wedges and serve from the casserole. Either way let it rest five or ten minutes after it leaves the oven.

At another table, Heaven popped a shrimp into her mouth. The Florida Seafood Council had conch, snapper, gulf shrimp and huge prawns prepared in all different ways. The California Produce Council had built a fruit salad the size of Delaware. A chocolate company was setting up a table in the shade to serve chocolate everything.

Lola smiled weakly. "Right now all I want is beans and rice and to be in my own kitchen. Heaven, I didn't get to thank you personally last night for your help. You really pulled it out of the fire for me, and I'll never forget it. One thing I must ask you, though. Do you trust your friend Bo Morales?"

"Lola, I know it looks bad for Bo. God knows, he's no angel. But I am sure Bo isn't the culprit this time."

"Because you know who is?"

"Trust me on this one, Lola. Now let me ask you one. Do you know anything personal about Linda Lunch? Or any dirt on the other nominees, things they would want to hide? Rack your brain."

Lola answered quickly. "Well, last year Tony La Sala worked for Norman Van Aken down in Miami, at Norman's. Norman was up here skiing and he came home mad as hell. Says Tony had two of his dishes on the menu, exactly the way Norman made them. But that's really all I know. Linda never came to Miami that I remember. I met her once in New York at the James Beard House. Everyone feared her but not more than they fear any of the other editors of the major food magazines. So that's not much."

Lola Castro shook hands formally with Heaven. "You and I know I don't stand a chance. But because of you I saved face. That's important for all the old girl cooks. We can't let the boys make us look like fools."

Heaven hugged Lola. "I don't see any old girls, here,

Lola. Good luck and I mean it. Come to Kansas City for a visit."

When she found Ernest Laveau he was attacking a plate of shrimp. Watching Ernest eat was not a pretty sight. He grabbed Heaven with a shrimpy hand. She quickly slipped out of his grasp, but gave him her best smile.

"Ernest, who knew we would get to be such good friends at this festival? What with the wreck and the murder and Lola's mess, we've been through a lot together."

Ernest winked at her. "You're OK for a white girl, Heaven, yes you are."

"What do you know about Linda Lunch? Anything that could help figure out who snapped her little neck?"

"I am proud to say I had never laid eyes on the little hussy until my accountant insisted I play along with this stupid Best Chef bullshit. He, my accountant, is fixin' to market a whole line of Marie Laveau's Voodoo spices for us and he wanted the press. As her great, great, great grandnephew I can use her name, don'tcha know."

"Your accountant was smart. Soon this will be just a distant memory and you'll be rackin' in the spice dough. But what's your instinct tell you?"

"There's some stinky cheese in Denmark when it comes to Sergio and Linda. Root around there."

"Good luck today. I'm gonna go find the La Salas."

"Good luck will be getting home alive. Come down for Jazz Fest, Heaven."

"Save a softshell crab po'boy for me," Heaven said as she set out to search for Sergio.

The awards stage sat on the very edge of the mountain. From it a string quartet was serenading the crowd. Heaven thought she recognized Dvorak. Cathedral Peak was directly behind and the music seemed to leave earth and become part of the heavens. For a moment Heaven's eyes involuntarily filled with tears of emotion. Classical music on a mountain was as close to a religious experience as Heaven had had in a long time.

Her reverie was shattered by Tony La Sala. He loomed in front of her, his usual nasty sneer in place.

"Today's my big day, Heaven. Today I whip my daddy's butt," Tony said with pride.

"What makes you so sure, asshole?" Heaven hissed. "Linda Lunch isn't cold yet, oops, poor choice of words, isn't stiff, isn't . . . you know what I mean, and all you can think about is some stupid triumph over your father."

"Easy for you to say, Heaven. I don't see your name on the Best Chef ballot."

"Tony, what's between your dad and Linda Lunch?"

Tony's face clouded and his eyes flashed with anger. Heaven felt the hair on her arms stick straight up. I hit a nerve, she thought.

"Nothing is between them," Tony said, "because that little tramp is dead."

" 'Little tramp'? You could say lots of things about Linda, but 'little tramp'? Why would you think that?"

"Just because she was old when she died doesn't mean she didn't tramp around in her youth. Everyone knows about her."

Heaven stared at him for a moment. "You're a loser. You'll lose today and unless a miracle occurs, you'll lose for the rest of your miserable life." Heaven walked off. His vibes were so bad she wondered how she could ever have hired him to work at her cafe.

Shaken by the encounter, she walked right into Sergio La Sala, who looked worse than he had when Heaven had found him on the floor of the cooking tent on Friday.

"Sergio, what happened to you?"

"How can you ask? After what's happened this weekend, with Linda gone . . ." his voice trailed off for a moment. "I don't know. I may never cook again. I have something to tell you, after the awards."

"Why not now?"

"Because I'm trying to keep myself together for a few more minutes. Don't worry. I won't jump off the mountain.

I want to tell you this, this secret. You're a strong person. I know you'll know what to do. I'll find you afterward," Sergio said and started to stumble off.

"Sergie," Heaven said, intentionally using the name she had heard Linda use. Sergio turned around, his eyes filled with tears. "Good luck today. You are the best chef of the bunch, you know that."

"None of it matters," he muttered as a group of festival goers surrounded him, telling him he would win and how much they liked his restaurant. Heaven slipped away.

Joe and Chris rushed to her side with Bo Morales in tow. "Heaven, hurry up. Go behind those trees over there and change into your waiter outfit. Tab is going to start in a minute." They were already in their little old lady outfits, gray wigs, white gloves, and flowered suit jackets.

Heaven grabbed the garment bag and Bo's hand. They found a hidden spot behind a tree and Heaven got out her Andy Warhol wig. "Help me put this thing on," she ordered Bo as she tied her hair back with a rubber hair band.

At that moment Bo leaned over and gave Heaven a real kiss, on the lips. For a second Heaven forgot what she had to do and just leaned into that kiss. Then she remembered, opened her eyes, and took a step back. Her lips were sticky with the fruits of rubbing two mouths together. She took a finger and wiped her lower lip, then smeared that stickiness between her breasts. "I'll just save that for later. Now put that wig on me and look me straight in the eye."

Bo started pulling the wig over Heaven's red tresses and pushed her hair up under the wig hairline. "I can feel a lecture coming on. Is this about the scam we pulled last year in Kansas City?" he asked.

"You've probably noticed some similarities. A national contest, a conspiracy to fix the winner. Swear on your most holy thing that you have not hurt the other Best Chef nominees."

Bo knew better than to joke now. "Heaven, I swear."

Heaven put on her waiter's coat and plastered on a fake

mustache. She stuck out her hand. "Shake on it?"

Bo shook. Heaven ran to the stage just as the ceremony was starting.

Tab welcomed everyone and gave a brief mourning speech about Linda, something about how Linda was an inspiration, how she had brought the food world to the rest of the world, how she would have wanted them to continue the festival. He asked everyone to make a toast to Linda Lunch. Everyone on the mountaintop held up a glass, including Joe and Chris who were on stage in their little old lady getups.

When the toast was over, the "girls" took over. They gave a hilarious account of their trip to the Cavern Club, gossiping about seeing various chefs and other celebrities. They pointed out cooks and winemakers in the audience and tossed off smart cracks about each of them. The crowd, desperate for a little levity after all the disasters, relaxed.

While Joe and Chris introduced all the Best Chef nominees, Heaven kibbitzed from the sidelines. The crowd loved it. When they introduced Tony, Heaven yelled out, "How about a caramel turtle, Tony?" a reference to his ill-fated meeting with Nathan Clark. Tony flushed and sat down quickly. The festival goers who had been in the Cavern Club on Friday night, or heard about the encounter, laughed and cheered.

When it was time for the first award, *The Real Dish* Best Dish, Heaven came up to the stage and joined Joe and Chris. Tab opened the envelope, which Heaven grabbed out of his hand. She glanced at it and went over to Sergio La Sala, and put the envelope up to her forehead as though she were Johnny Carson playing The Great Karnak.

"The winner of *The Real Dish* Best Dish was born in San Francisco, California, in 1966. Sergio, name that winner!"

Sergio looked at Heaven with something akin to relief in his eyes. I was right, Heaven thought. Good for me. She had relieved Tab of his cordless mike when she relieved him of the envelope and she now stuck the microphone in Sergio's face. He paused and looked over at his son, who looked even

wilder and more dangerous than he had a few minutes ago.
Then Sergio said, "Then the winner is my son, Tony. Congratulations, son."

The crowd warmly responded. Even those who hadn't
known about the family feud had certainly heard about it by
now. A reconciliation might not be possible, but a dad wishing his son well was the second best thing.

But Tony stood rigidly, staring poison darts at his dad.
Heaven moved in for the kill. "Yes, Sergio is right. Tony
La Sala wins the Best Dish award, and what a dish it was.
For those of you not fortunate enough to have been at the
dinner last night, Tony served the first course, a pureed potato soup with truffle oil, combined with a rich mushroom
broth, Parmesan shavings, and sliced truffles on the top. It
was magnificent. The only trouble is that it wasn't Tony's
dish."

The crowd made a collective noise, something between an
oooh and a groan. Heaven went on, moving as far away from
Tony as was possible on the tiny stage, and pulling two
sheets of paper out of her jacket pocket. "I called Boston
this morning and talked to Todd English, the chef owner of
Olives. He was very interested in hearing what Tony cooked
last night and sent me these two faxes. One is a menu from
Charlie Trotter's James Beard dinner last year, and the other
is from a state dinner at the White House that Boston chefs
cooked in February of this year. Guess what? The soup
course on each menu was a potato soup with mushroom
broth, truffles, and Parmesan shavings. I'm just going to give
these to Tab Garner, Linda's able assistant. You all are welcome to examine them yourself. In the meantime, I think *The
Real Dish* better find a new Best Dish." Tony La Sala had
vanished. Heaven moved to the side of the stage and handed
the mike to Tab. The crowd was going wild.

Tab opened his mouth, but nothing came out. He smiled
weakly and tried again. "Well, this has been the weekend
of surprises and at this point, nothing surprises me. I'm going
to ask my colleague from the business office who tabulated

the results to come forward and let us know who was second in the voting.'' Tab looked around the crowd frantically. A young MBA-type pushed forward. There was a whispered consultation.

Tab turned to the crowd with a big smile on his face. ''The new winner of the Best Dish award is also the winner of the overall Best Chef award. Sergio La Sala!''

The crowd rose to give Sergio a standing ovation. He came up and said a few poignant words about the award meaning more because he had waited so many years for it. Then he walked away.

Tab, wondering what else could go wrong, wound up the ceremony quickly. He hadn't seen the Best Dish fiasco coming. Heaven must have known about Tony when they were at breakfast. Of course, he didn't blame her for not sharing the information. He hadn't given her one reason to trust him.

Heaven worked her way over to Sergio who was surrounded by well-wishers. When she finally caught his eye, he excused himself and came toward her.

''I think Tony knows,'' Sergio said.

Heaven nodded. ''You think he knows that Linda was his mother?''

Sergio looked at her tentatively, not knowing where to start. ''We had been fighting about it for years. Linda didn't want to tell him, then she did. I didn't want to tell him, then I did. But we never agreed. If I was gung-ho, she said it was out of the question, and vice-versa. Then about three months ago, Linda called me and said we had to tell Tony. She wouldn't be straight with me about why she was so determined all of a sudden. But she did say that it was for his own good. Now that scared me. How could finding out your mother wasn't dead but was a woman who hadn't wanted anything to do with you, be good for a kid?''

''So you tried to put Linda off?'' Heaven asked.

''I insisted that we wait until the festival was over. I hadn't spoken to Tony for years. I guess I thought we might, being here together . . . I wanted to give it a chance first. What if

Tony and I had made up and then he found out that everything I'd told him about his mother was a lie?''

"Was that enough of a threat to make you kill his
mother?'' Heaven asked.

Sergio shook his head vehemently. ''What would be the
point? You know Tony had no intention of making up with
me. You were at the party on Thursday. Don't get me wrong.
There were many times I wanted to wring Linda's neck myself. On the way to the party she taunted me, said wouldn't
Tony be surprised that his mother wasn't some Italian saint
but a San Francisco sinner.

"That probably wasn't the approach you had in mind for
a family reunion.''

Sergio leaned up against a tree, rubbing the stitches on his
head from Friday's attack. ''I thought I had her talked into
waiting until today. I said we could sit down, the three of
us, after this stupid awards thing was out of the way and tell
him together. But she must have gone behind my back for
her own reasons. Linda has never been easy to figure out.''

Heaven gave him a little hug. ''How did you end up with
Linda and then with your kid?''

"When I met Linda in San Francisco, I lied. I told her I
had a wife in Italy. I didn't. It was a cheap trick, I know.
But I didn't want her or anyone to get serious about me. So
I lied. When Linda became pregnant, I confessed that I
wasn't really married and told her I wanted to make an honest woman of her. But she hated me for lying to her all those
months. Said she'd felt all that guilt about having an affair
with a married man for nothing. She told me she would put
our baby up for adoption, that I'd never see it. I'm a good
Catholic boy, or I was then. I was frantic. She tortured me
but in the end she let me have our baby on the condition that
he never know who his mother was. Said she didn't want to
have anything to do with him or me. So I went back to the
wife in Italy story.'' He looked at Heaven. ''How did you
figure it out?''

"I didn't as much figure it out as back into it. It was

obvious that something serious was going on between you and Linda. Rowland told me that you two had a grudge from way back. You had the kid and the mom had mysteriously died in childbirth in Italy. There was plenty of room for a fertile imagination to put two and two together. Today at the awards announcement, I thought if I said he was born in San Francisco and he really was born in Italy it wouldn't hurt anyone and I'd get to see your reactions.''

''And my reaction was to recognize who you were talking about. I could argue that it was merely process of elimination. None of the rest of the candidates could have been born in 1966. But I'm tired of the lies. You sure took a cheap shot out there, when you busted Tony's soup. How could you do it? Tony must be humiliated.''

''Tony has to be stopped. I figured there was a chance he wouldn't win, and then I wouldn't have said a thing. But Tony is ruthless. We can't have these young kids think they can build their reputations on other cooks' food. I'm not sorry I did it. That's not the bad part.''

''What's the bad part?''

''I think either you or Tony killed Linda Lunch.''

Sergio shook his head sadly. ''I don't know how you got to that conclusion. I pray that you're wrong because I know it wasn't me. I still loved the woman.'' With that Sergio walked away in the direction of the gondolas. Heaven didn't try to stop him.

TWENTY-NINE

"SO, do we have a plan?" Heaven asked, looking at the assembled group.

Joe nodded. "I'm going to help Bo pack up and load his chuckwagon. Chris and Tab are going to finish up here and then go down to the police station so Tab can confess that he's been playing dirty tricks. Rowland has to go to the airport so he can be at a wine dinner in Cleveland tomorrow. You're going to the grocery store after you bop by the police station and tell them about Sergio, Linda, and Tony. We'll all meet at the house and have dinner with Trixie Malone, everyone but Rowland, of course, who will already be winging his way to Cleveland." Joe turned to Rowland. "Cleveland has never sounded as good. I think I speak for everyone when I say we can't get out of town fast enough."

Rowland Alexander shook hands all around, until he got to Heaven who he scooped close under his arm one last time. "I knew bringing you to *The Real Dish* festival was going to be an exciting experience. I just didn't realize how exciting."

Heaven laughed. "I can see how the story is shaping up already. This whole thing is going to be my fault by next week. Rowland, the next time you need some acting done, call the Screen Actors Guild or Equity. Have a safe trip, honey."

"Ride down with me?" Rowland asked.

Heaven shook her head. "I'm about to burst. I have to run into the ladies' room. I'll be down in a few minutes. Don't wait."

"We'll go with Rowland," Joe said, and he and Bo and Rowland headed for the gondolas. Chris and Tab were already busy somewhere.

Heaven thought wistfully of riding down in the gondola with Rowland and having a mad, passionate necking session. Murders always made Heaven feel reckless. "Resisting temptation seems silly in the face of how brief our time on earth is," Heaven said to the mountains.

She was on autopilot, using the ladies' room, trying the phone to call Murray and getting no answer, and heading toward the gondola again. The crowd of festival goers had long since departed, eager to hit the wine tasting tent one last time. The roundhouse attendant wasn't in sight and the gondola launching pad was empty. Heaven absently climbed in a gondola. It took almost a minute for the gondola to move through the roundhouse and turn itself around for the trip back to Aspen, and Heaven was a million miles away. She was replaying the conversation with Sergio. Would Sergio kill to prevent Linda from telling Tony the truth? A sudden lurch of the gondola brought her back. She looked around, thinking the gondola was leaving the roundhouse. But what she saw was Tony La Sala.

"I was getting worried, you witch. I thought you'd flown down the mountain on your broomstick." Tony must have waited until the last possible moment before jumping into the gondola. He wedged his foot in the door to keep it open and reached for Heaven's neck with one hand. In his other hand was a particularly nasty-looking boning knife.

Heaven tried to ignore her rising pulse rate. "What's the matter with you?" she asked. "Are you crazy? It's not like you won't be caught at the end of the cable line. We're on a cable car with only one way to go, down to civilization. Why don't you just throw that knife out the door?"

"Oh, I'll throw something out the door, Heaven, but it won't be the knife. No, the knife is just a little persuader." He grabbed Heaven's hair and pulled her head back, craning her neck to the perfect throat-cutting position.

Heaven gasped and fought to breathe. "If you're not going to kill me with that knife, what are you going to do? Wait. Don't answer that."

Tony stroked the blade against Heaven's neck, the dull side touching her skin. "Why did you do that to me, you fucking bitch? My dish was the Best Dish. It was voted so by the people who ate the fucking dinner. I beat my father. I beat them all. I was the best and you ruined it. It's none of your business if I made a dish like Todd English or Nathan Clark or Norman Van Aken. What's it to you?"

Heaven wasn't going to argue at this point or suggest that stealing, even if it was just recipes, was bad. "You're right," she said. "I should have stayed out of it, and I'll be out of your hair soon. You can go back to wowing the movie stars in Aspen and I'll go back to boring old Kansas City."

"Not so fast. You're not going anywhere except out the door. You're just another lying, meddling bitch."

Heaven was afraid she was going to hear something she didn't want to hear. If Tony confessed to the murder of Linda Lunch, Heaven's chances of getting off the gondola alive evaporated completely. She was staring ahead, her only option at this point, thanks to the knife. Not too far in front of her and to her left was the end of the line for the Bell Mountain lift. Heaven remembered from when she was talking to Chris earlier that this area looked fairly close to the ground, at least compared to the gorge on either side. This area of the mountain was where a whole group of black ski runs were located, the most difficult ski runs on steeper terrain. Heaven knew that after that one spot ahead, the cable towers for the gondola were at least one hundred feet from the ground. She knew she had to get out of the gondola almost immediately, when she had a chance of just breaking a leg or arm.

"Tony, I'm afraid of heights. How far up are we any-how?"

Tony jerked on her hair. "Good, bitch. I'm glad you're afraid. You should be afraid. We're somewhere around ten thousand feet now. Does that sound like a good place to die? No one is coming up the mountain and I made sure no one was in the gondolas behind us. When I push you out, I'll have plenty of time to get down the mountain, then go to the club, and start the prep for dinner. Tonight someone will be at the bar talking about how that stupid bitch from Kansas City fell out of a gondola and broke her neck."

With that Tony jerked on Heaven's shoulder while trying to force open the swivel door with his foot and leg. Because he couldn't continue holding the knife so close to her throat, Heaven realized it was worth a shot. She lunged forward and slipped her left arm through the space between the railing and the round window. Tony was enraged.

"Fine, Heaven. I'll pull your body out the door and leave your arm dangling there." The door was open enough now for someone to fall out and the gondola was swinging wildly back and forth. They were swinging in such a wide arc, Heaven was sure they were going to crash into the next cable tower.

"Let go!" Tony screamed at her and brought the knife down in the soft, underside of her arm with a slashing motion. Heaven looked away quickly. She didn't have the option of fainting. But she caught a glimpse of the flesh separating like it did when she boned a turkey breast. The idea of jumping was looking better every moment. As Tony's hand rose to slash her again, she let go of the rail, swung her legs toward the open door and pushed Tony with all her might. The element of surprise was hers and Tony lost his balance. The next thing she knew, he was gone, the knife glinting as it flew through the air catching the afternoon sun. Heaven was hanging half out of the door, her legs squashed as the automatic closure device activated. She eased herself back inside, letting the door close, then got up on her knees on the seat and peered out.

Her idea of a good place to jump must have been right because Tony was lying on the ground, but still moving. Heaven could see blood on his face, but she didn't know if it was his or hers. Then he got up and limped toward the woods, glaring up at her.

She looked down at her arm. The blood was flowing.

"Where are you supposed to put the pressure?" Heaven asked aloud. "Closer to the heart." She drew her arm into her body, holding it as tight as she could above the elbow and doubled over as if she had a stomach ache. "I wish I'd kept that damn waiter's coat on. I hate bare arms. I can't even remember where all our stuff . . . oh, yeah. Joe took it."

Heaven rocked back and forth now, trying not to look at all the blood. She figured she had about five minutes before she'd be down the mountain. It was time to start humming. Rocking and humming. She was so tired. Maybe the time would go faster if she just sat down on the floor and rested. She kept humming and rocking until her gondola went over the rise and she could see Aspen below.

Then she slipped down on the floor and tried to curl up in a fetal position. It felt so good to lie down. She would just close her eyes for a minute.

THIRTY

"SO, do we have another plan?" Heaven was rubbing her bandaged arm. Her stitches already itched.

Bo Morales put his arm around Heaven and gently pulled her hand away from the gauze and tape. He led her to his pickup truck in the hospital parking lot. "Let's hope it's better than that last one. Yes, we have a plan already in action. Joe took your car and went to the grocery store. He was going home to intercept the movie star or at least tell her to come down around seven. I called the hotel and told my brother and the rest of the team they were on their own packing up. Mercedes says 'feel better.' She's leaving us a box of barbecue at the Ritz's front desk for appetizers. We'll just swing by and pick that up. Joe said he was going to make a one-dish meal.

"While you were in with the doc, I talked to Officer Rainey. They're looking for Tony everywhere.

"He also said they weren't keeping Tab and throwing away the key. No one will press charges. The publisher spent an hour at the police station; he doesn't want more bad publicity. I guess the nominees were all consulted too. Ernest said all he wanted was to never hear about *The Real Dish* magazine again. Lola came over and talked to Tab and left him in tears, promising to pray for him. Sergio is still there. I guess they have moved on to the murder investigation. Anyway, Tab and Chris will be done soon. Heaven, you've never let me talk this long without interrupting. You haven't made a peep.''

"I'm drugged, so you better enjoy the quiet. You probably have until tomorrow morning before I get sassy again.''

Bo leaned over and gave Heaven a kiss on the cheek. "Does that mean I might have a chance to be around in the morning?'' He grinned wickedly and opened the truck door for Heaven.

"Just because I'm weak doesn't mean I'm easy,'' Heaven said, trying to joke.

Bo stopped the truck at the front door of the Ritz. "No one would call you that, Heaven. I'll be right back.''

While Bo was in the hotel, Heaven found herself jumping every time a passerby neared the truck. She was spooked, there was no doubt about it. Thank goodness she hadn't actually seen Tony falling through space. Not that the memory of a knife slashing down wasn't enough material for nightmares. She started to shudder. Heaven took a long breath. "Breathe deep,'' she told herself. She had a few more Demerols in her pocket and she intended to use them. The doctor had tried to give her Tylenol Threes, but she would have none of it. She had demanded something stronger. Reality was not an option right now. Especially since Tony was still running around loose. She started shaking just as Bo climbed back in the truck. He said nothing, but held her until the shakes stopped.

As they made their way up the mountain, Bo tried small talk. "So, what's this Trixie Malone like?''

Heaven smiled. "We met Trixie when she was chasing after her Pekinese, a disgusting little creature who loves to swim. She, Trixie, not the dog, was ditzy but nice. Since fate handed us a movie star, I thought we should try to make a good impression on her. After all, Joe and Chris are in show-biz. It couldn't hurt for them to be friends with a big star. Hey, maybe tonight will be your lucky break, too, Bo.''

Bo looked over at Heaven hopefully and put his hand on

her leg. "That's what I was angling for at the hospital. We could let the guys entertain Trixie, and we could turn in early. You need your rest."

"I was referring to your ambition to be a movie star, which we all agree you will be someday soon. I've seen the way those barbecue groupies look at you. I think you should be nice to Trixie tonight and give her that million-watt smile. Stop here at the guard station. I have to sign us in."

The ski hunk was on duty tonight. "Hello there, Ms. Lee. I'm glad to see you. I just came on duty and was checking the sign-in sheets for the day. Chris's signature doesn't look anything like his previous signatures. I was going to call up there."

Suddenly Heaven felt sober, the pleasant numbness from the drugs gone. Next came the adrenaline rush. Chris shouldn't be here at all. He was supposed to be with Tab at the police station. Of course, it was possible that he had come up to the house to get something. Or maybe he just got tired of hanging around the police station waiting for a guy he barely knew. Somehow Heaven didn't buy any of these possibilities.

The guard passed the sheet over to Heaven. She signed it. It definitely wasn't Chris's handwriting. According to this, Joe was also at the house. She saw his neat left-handed John Hancock at the bottom of the page. She didn't want to tell the guard the truth about the fake Chris until she made sure the real Joe was OK.

Heaven smiled across Bo at the hunk. Bo rolled his eyes. He was getting as good as her staff at seeing one of her lies coming. "Well, we had a couple of crises today and maybe Chris wasn't a hundred percent. I do agree with you that it doesn't look like Chris's usual signature and I'm very impressed that someone actually compares these things to the originals. No wonder this place is so famous. There is the possibility that Chris had a little too much wine. We have been at a wine festival, you know."

"Let me know if you need me," the guard said as he handed Bo his card.

Bo nodded. "If you don't hear from us, everything is OK. And thank you again."

As they pulled away from the guardhouse, Bo asked "What's the deal?"

"That wasn't Chris's signature, but it was Joe's. We may have a real Joe and a fake Chris and after today, I'm a little paranoid. Can you think of anyone who would want to be Chris for any legitimate reason?"

Bo turned into the Cooper drive. There was a Range Rover parked in the drive as well. Heaven started to open her door and fell back against Bo. "Whoa, the drugs have kicked back in. Here's what we'll do. I'll go in, and you sneak around to the back."

Bo opened his door and walked around to help Heaven. "The back of this house is a sheer drop. I don't think sneaking in that way is going to work this time, honey. You think it's Tony, don't you?"

"Who else would bother?"

"I guess we'll find out. I think this time we're just going to have to meet the enemy head-on. Joe may need us."

Heaven shook her head. "Meet the enemy head-on? That's not our style. There is a side yard with a lap pool on the east side. Maybe I can climb over the fence and . . ."

"Please. I know you love being macho, but this time you're high on Demerol. Let's just take it easy," Bo said as he pushed the front door open. "It wasn't pulled shut. That's not a good sign."

Just then, they heard laughter from the kitchen. Feminine laughter. Rich, deep feminine laughter. They followed that laughter and found Tony La Sala and Trixie Malone, drinking wine and having a great old time.

"Hi, you two," Heaven said faintly.

Tony looked up and gave Heaven a mocking salute with his wine glass. Then he put down the wine and picked up a huge Chinese cleaver and resumed chopping some onions.

Trixie spoke first, still making goo-goo eyes at Tony. "I just stopped by when I came from town to find out what time for dinner." Trixie patted her hair, which was perfect, just like her makeup. "And Tony was already here cooking up a storm. The boy just wouldn't let me leave. I always love going to the club and I've just been raving to everyone at home about you, Tony. Will you come to L.A. and cook for a party for me, sugar?"

"I'd go anywhere with you, Trixie," Tony said with his trademark sneer and a knowing look directed at Heaven.

It wasn't until this moment that Trixie turned toward the kitchen door and spotted Bo Morales. She stood up and straightened her painted-on lipstick-red North Beach leather suit. "Heaven, I realize that I have underestimated you. Somehow you have the hottest chef in town up here chopping and dicing for you. Then you come home with this, this Adonis. Have we met in L.A.? You look familiar," Trixie purred as she glided across the floor toward Bo, her hand extended.

Heaven and Bo had been frozen in the doorway, assessing the situation. It wasn't good. When Trixie started toward Bo, Tony moved around on the side of the counter nearest her, the cleaver still in his hand and his eyes on Heaven and Bo. Of course, Trixie couldn't see what was going on behind her back. She could barely see Heaven since she was so focused on Bo. It was a trick that had served her well over the years. Heaven and Bo walked slowly toward Tony, with Trixie in between.

Suddenly Heaven felt another case of the shakes coming on. She sat down at the kitchen table. Tackling Tony was out of the question right now. She would just have to try talking him out of whatever he had in mind. "Trixie, you're learning that I'm just full of surprises. Tony, I wasn't sure if you'd be able to make it. I heard you took a fall today. Oh, I forgot my manners. Trixie Malone, meet Bo Morales, the handsomest man in all of Texas. Bo was one of the nominees for Best Chef at the festival this year."

Trixie took Bo's hand in both of hers. "Bo Morales, is it? So, Bo, did you win?"

Tony broke in. "No, my old man was the winner, after all these years."

Bo led Trixie to the table and sat her beside Heaven, then turned his back on Tony as if he wasn't a threat. He calmly walked over to the counter and got Trixie's wine glass. "Sergio La Sala is a legend, as you are, Miss Malone. It was an honor just to be in his company."

Heaven had done her deep breathing for a minute and was ready to spell Bo. She got up and took two wine glasses from the bar. "There's a bottle of Cloudy Bay Sauvignon Blanc," she said, opening the bar refrigerator. "How does that sound, Bo? What are you guys drinking?"

Tony was sautéing onions. What was this maniac up to? Heaven wondered.

"There was a great vintage of Heitz, Martha's Vineyard, Cabernet Sauvignon on the rack, Heaven. I just helped myself," Tony said from the stove.

"By the way, where is Joe?" Heaven asked. "I thought he was coming home with the groceries."

Tony turned and grinned at Heaven. "The groceries were here all right, but I don't see Joe, do you? Maybe he got tied up."

Heaven glanced at Bo, who had also caught Tony's little play on words. Again she went to the refrigerator and peered in. "Darn. Bo, we forgot the barbecue in the car. Why don't you and Trixie go out and get it? Trixie, Bo is a barbecue king and he does all his cooking in a turn-of-the-century chuckwagon. It's just fascinating."

Bo looked intensely at Heaven for a second, then got up and took Trixie's hand. "Good idea," he said, and headed for the door, pulling Trixie a little too fast for the three-inch heels she was wearing.

"Whoa, Bo, honey. Slow down a little," Trixie said as she teetered after Bo.

Just then they heard the front door opening and Chris and Tab talking.

Bo pushed Trixie in the direction of the living room and yelled at her, "Run, Trixie. Tell them to call the guards. Run."

Trixie hesitated just a minute, like a good film star would do so the camera could see the wheels turning in her pretty little head. Is he serious? Did he really say what I thought he said? That playing to the camera cost Trixie valuable time. That and the three-inch high heels meant that Tony La Sala caught up with Trixie in the middle of the living room.

Tony got past Bo and Heaven by grabbing Heaven by her bad arm and throwing her toward Bo. Heaven yelped in pain and Bo instinctively reached out to help her, another move that cost valuable time.

Chris and Tab heard Bo yell and came running from the other side of the house. They didn't stand a chance of getting to Trixie before Tony did. Tony tackled Trixie and pinned her to the floor.

"Don't run or I'll chop her head off and it won't be in one blow," Tony screeched, Chinese cleaver in his hand.

Bo and Heaven were at one door. Bo was trying to estimate the distance between the door and Tony. Heaven was trying not to scream from the pain in her arm.

Chris and Tab were at the other door. They were behind the learning curve on what was going down, but they were catching up fast. Chris was trying to figure out how to make it back to the front door. Tab, who had taken kick-boxing last year, was picturing the top of Tony's head meeting his hiking boot.

Tony and Trixie were in the living room, which now looked like the main arena of a mixed gender wrestling match. Tony was breathing hard and making a high-pitched whine. Trixie was ready to see if she could act her way out of a dangerous situation.

When Trixie opened her mouth, she had acquired a Southern accent. Georgia, Heaven guessed. "Tony, what the devil are you doing, sugar? Why, I was havin' such a nice visit with you and then everyone came home and just spoiled it, didn't they, sugar?''

Tony held the cleaver closer to her throat. He was lying on top of her and pulling her head back in a way that Heaven knew only too well. ''No deal, Trixie, I know that one. *Black Cherry Blues*, 1994. You played the role Kim Basinger walked out on. Nice job.''

''Tony, what do you want?'' Heaven asked. ''I don't think you came up here to scare the shit out of Trixie Malone.'' She stuck her hand in her jeans pocket for the Demerol. She was almost faint with the pain.

Tony shook his head wildly. ''You've ruined my life. Now I'm going to ruin yours. Or you can get Trixie and me out of Aspen in one piece. Let's just call it a hostage situation.''

''Can I call the police and have them send a hostage negotiator?'' Heaven asked innocently as she swallowed two pills.

''Don't anyone go near that telephone. No cell phones, either. Let me see your hands. Everybody put their hands up so I can see them,'' Tony ordered.

Heaven had to pull on Bo's jacket to let him know he was going to have to help her to her feet. She had the look of a pain-crazed bull elephant, but her voice was smooth as silk. ''Tony, nobody is concealing a cellular phone, much less a weapon of destruction. Calm down. Taking hostages is frowned on. Of course, what you did to Linda won't exactly win you the best son award but before you acted the fool with me and pinned Trixie, I had a hunch what happened with Linda was an accident.''

''Best son?'' Tab squawked from the other side of the room. ''You must be kidding. Don't tell me Linda was . . .''

''Shut up!'' Tony screamed. ''Will you just shut up about Linda? Can you believe that bitch? All this time I thought I had some sainted mother. I thought Sergio hated me for being born and his beloved old-country wife for dying. Then I find out that the whole thing was a lie. Do you know what

Linda said? What her actual words were? '*I'm* your mother. Your mother wasn't some Italian bitch.' ''

''And that's when you choked her?'' Heaven asked, trying to sound understanding.

''No, I asked what she was talking about. She said old Sergio and her were an item when he landed in San Francisco.''

Heaven tried again. ''At least she didn't have an abortion, Tony.''

Tony responded by pulling Trixie's head back even further. ''Then she told me she would never have let me know the truth, but she had a hereditary disease, something called lupus. She said it might kill her and I'd probably get it in a few years.''

''Linda could always kill with a word,'' Tab said.

Heaven jumped in again. ''Lupus isn't always fatal, Tony. I have a friend who has it and she does just fine. She's learned to control it with diet and . . .''

''Shut up!'' Tony yelped.

''I can't breathe,'' Trixie yelped.

Tony waved the cleaver menacingly. ''Linda still didn't care. She was just telling me so she could torture me. 'Hello, son. Your whole life is a lie and not only that, it may kill you in the end. By the way, you better let your father win tonight, scorch your soup or something. If you don't,' she said, 'I'll spill the beans about your true origins, which are more trailer park than Lake Como.' '' Tony let out a choked sob.

Trixie looked helplessly up at Tab and Chris. She strained to speak. ''Am I hearing right? You killed someone named Linda who was your mother? And you didn't know until yesterday she was your mother? And she gave you a genetic defect?''

''Shut up!'' Tony screamed again.

Heaven sensed they were making headway. ''Her neck was broken, Tony. You didn't take a weapon with you, for God's sake. It's not like it was premeditated," Heaven cooed. "What did she say that made you choke her so hard?"

Tony put his head on Trixie's shoulder for a second, as though he was trying to remember. "I never wanted you," he said in a very good imitation of Linda Lunch's voice.

"Poor thing," Heaven said. "That's the phrase you'll hear ringing in your ears for the rest of your life."

"Crime of passion," Tab offered.

Bo sensed it before it actually happened. Heaven felt him tense up.

Trixie Malone had had enough. When she felt Tony relax slightly, she reached back and grabbed Tony's groin area. At the same time she bucked, trying to throw him off her back.

Tab quickly moved into action and kicked at Tony La Sala with all his might. Tony didn't know where to grab first: the hellion under him, the boot flying into him for a second blow, or his own private parts.

Trixie yelped when the cleaver knicked her hand as it clanked to the floor. That served as a signal for a free-for-all in the middle of the living room. Everyone except Heaven jumped into the fray. Chris dove in, trying to pull Trixie out from under Tony. Tony tried to dodge the tips of Bo's custom-made eel cowboy boots and Tab's hiking boots. Heaven just turned back into the kitchen, the pain pills kicking in.

"I think I'll just call our friend the guard. Or maybe 911 and then the guard," she said to no one in particular. "Then I'll go try to find Joe. I guess he's tied up somewhere."

THIRTY-ONE

JOE got up and passed the bowl around again. It was his 1990's version of tuna noodle casserole and it was delicious. The noodles were cooked in a creamy sauce studded with mushrooms, calamata olives, and toasted pine nuts. A chunky piece of rare roasted tuna perched on top of each serving of pasta. They found some spicy Rhone reds to drink with it, a Cornas and a Cotes du Rhone. It took a group of foodies to still be hungry after all the excitement they'd been through tonight.

Joe's Tuna Noodle Update

tuna steaks, six ounces per person
1 lb. fettucine noodles, boiled and oiled
1 cup calamata olives, pitted
1 lb. white mushrooms, sliced
1 cup pine nuts, lightly toasted
1 10-oz. package frozen peas or 1 cup blanched snow
 peas
butter
olive oil
kosher salt and white pepper
cream
chicken stock

1 cup bleu cheese or gorgonzola, crumbled
Italian parsley

The tuna steaks should be grilled or roasted very
simply, with a little oil and kosher salt. This shouldn't
take more than ten minutes so get your sauce done first.
Heat 3 T. butter in a large sauté pan. Slowly sauté
the mushrooms that have been sliced. When they are
fully cooked, sprinkle the mushrooms with flour until
you have a loose paste that has absorbed most of the
moisture. Cook for five minutes. Add 2 cups each,
stock and cream. Stir and simmer to thicken. Add olives, cheese, and peas that have been defrosted by rinsing with warm water in a colander. Season with salt
and pepper. Add pine nuts at the last minute. After the
sauce is medium thick, the last steps should be taken
quickly. Serve in a heated pasta bowl with the tuna
steak on the top. Garnish with more pine nuts and
sprigs of Italian parsley.

It was almost midnight. After killing his mother in a rage,
trying to kill Heaven, falling twenty feet out of a ski gondola,
taking a movie star hostage and getting kicked with a thou-
sand-dollar cowboy boot, all in one twenty-four-hour period,
Tony was through. Before the police arrived, Tony just lay
on the floor, not struggling, with Tab sitting on him. He was
taken into custody and left without saying another word.

None of them were feeling in top form. Tab had lost his
job and his future in magazine publishing. Chris had fallen
hard for Tab, only to discover that the guy was dishonest.
Joe had been gagged and tied up in the closet. And Heaven
had a nasty cut that would leave a scar to remind her of
Tony forever.

Bo Morales might have suffered the most burdensome pre-
dicament. He had a beautiful movie star who was in between
husbands convinced he had saved her life. Like the Chinese
proverb about someone saving your life and you being re-

sponsible for them for the rest of their life, Trixie had been plastered on Bo since she got out from under Tony. Bo was uncomfortable but intrigued. Trixie had a cute little bandage on her hand where the cleaver had fallen.

"So, Heaven, you think he came up to get you?" Tab asked.

"Well, I don't think he snuck in here just to see Trixie Malone or confess his crime of passion. You can't really blame him. I exposed him as a fraud in front of the whole festival and then pushed him out of a gondola. You wouldn't like me either," Heaven said wearily.

Tab checked his watch and then stood up. He raised his glass for a toast. "It's midnight, and I officially proclaim this nightmare over. May all our future Junes be spent far from Aspen, Colorado."

"Hear, hear," the group said solemnly.

"And may all our Christmases be white," Heaven added, hoping everyone would leave.

Trixie draped herself decoratively over Bo's shoulder. "Bo, honey, would you go up to the house with me? I'm still a little shook. I don't want to go in that big house alone after what we went through tonight."

The whole table turned to look at Heaven, and not very subtly either. Bo had a question in his eyes: If I go home with Trixie Malone, will I ruin my friendship with Heaven and any future chances of something more? Everyone else had a question in their eyes too: Is she going to kill him or her?

She surprised everyone. Heaven got up and kissed each of them on the cheek. "I'm turning into a pumpkin, but I think I can still make it to the phone to call my daughter in England. We always try to call on Sundays and it's already Monday morning there. Bo, take care of Miss Malone. Tab, don't keep Chris up too late. We have a long drive tomorrow."

She left them all speechless.

When Heaven got in bed, she dialed her daughter's number. Iris had been in England for three years, going to Oxford and living with her rock-star father. It was almost time for her to come home for the summer. "Hi, honey. How was my weekend in Aspen? You won't believe it, honey. I'll give you the headlines now and the details when you get home. Which will be before July Fourth, I hope. I miss you, Iris. I need you to come home, now."

THIRTY-TWO

"I'VE got the last bags from upstairs," Joe yelled as he headed down the grand staircase.

"And I've got the Robo-Coupe," Heaven yelled from the kitchen where she was filling their cooler with ice from the restaurant-size icemaker.

Joe peered in at her, his disapproving expression like an old maid librarian's.

"Just kidding," Heaven cracked. She was amazed at how good she felt. Maybe it was because they were going home to Kansas City.

Joe leaned up against the door. "Are you mad about or at Bo?"

Heaven shoved a six-pack of Diet Dr Pepper in the ice and closed the cooler, lifting it and heading for the door. "I thought about that last night. Not that I, who live with the most wonderful guy in Kansas City, has the right to be jealous and possessive of Bo."

Joe grinned as they walked out to the van. "But that's never stopped you before."

Chris's head stuck out of the back of the van. He was the loading expert. "Give me the garment bags first, then the cooler. Joe, take the last run through the house while I get us organized. Heaven, did you get your purse?"

As Joe and Heaven turned toward the house for the final

run-through, a bright red Ferrari pulled up in the drive. Trixie Malone and Bo Morales, both wearing glamorous sunglasses, waved. Bo jumped out and pulled Heaven aside.

"Heaven, I don't know what to say. Do you hate me?"

Heaven punched him on the arm playfully. He responded by lifting her bandaged limb gently to his lips and kissing her hand in his usual corny way.

"Don't be silly," Heaven said. "I'm the one who told you to be nice to her and maybe it would be your lucky movie star break."

Bo ducked his head bashfully. "Actually she's already offered me a nice part. We start filming in the fall, after the barbecue season is over. But, Heaven, you and I have been through so much together. I couldn't feel closer to you if we were really, if we . . . you know what I mean."

"Yes, I do know what you mean. We have a long life ahead of us, Bo. We're solid. Now go, have fun, get famous," Heaven said as she pushed him toward the car and Trixie. She was amazed at her own fairness and even temper. Losing a suitor like Bo to a gorgeous movie star would normally be the perfect excuse for a diva fit. Could it be the Demerol?

Cafe Heaven was packed. Monday night was open mike night and the midtown Kansas City crowd showed up to see what favorite band or poet or playwright was trying out new material.

Murray Steinblatz was beaming. So far not one single thing had gone wrong at the restaurant today.

Heaven, Chris, and Joe had called Murray at home before leaving Aspen earlier that morning. Murray almost spilled the beans about Jack's episode and the Auto Club inspection team. But before he could get it out, Heaven told Murray about Tony La Sala and Tony's mother and Heaven's ride down the mountain with Tony and her knife wound. He just couldn't bother her with Cafe Heaven problems after that. And besides, he reasoned, Mona was walking just fine and

Jack was lucid and the Auto Club inspectors, well, there wasn't a thing any of them could do about the Auto Club inspectors. So Murray told Heaven everything was fine and to drive carefully and he would see them all on Tuesday. He knew Heaven would yell at him for holding out on her, but he could take it. He felt much braver after the last five days.

Murray glanced at his watch. It was time to start the show. He went up on the tiny stage and let out a Bronx whistle to get the attention of the room. "Good evening, folks. Welcome to Cafe Heaven open mike night. We've got such a great lineup for you tonight, you won't even notice that Chris and Joe are MIA, missing in Aspen, this week." The crowd groaned at Murray's bad pun. He grinned. "But before I introduce our first player tonight, I have something I want to share with you. It's a piece I wrote. Actually it's the first thing I've written in a few years. I hope you'll forgive my rusty metaphors." Murray took a couple of folded sheets of paper out of his pocket and straightened them out. "The name of this piece is 'Fear of Heights,' " Murray said with a little quiver in his voice. Then he began reading.